# DEVIL'S DEAL

## ALEATHA ROMIG

*NEW YORK TIMES BESTSELLING AUTHOR*

New York Times, Wall Street Journal, and USA Today
bestselling author of the Consequences, Infidelity, and
Sparrow Web series: Web of Sin, Tangled Web, Web of
Desire, and Dangerous Web

# COPYRIGHT AND LICENSE INFORMATION

2021 Edition License

# DEVIL'S DEAL

What is your desire?
Lust, money, or power?

I am the man who can make every dream come true, for a price.

Years ago, a fight for supremacy took place between the two most powerful families in New Orleans. The battle was set in the metaphoric octagon with the spotlight blazing. The city sat in paralyzed fear, awaiting word of a victor.

Abraham Ramses versus Isaiah Boudreau.
One man would emerge victorious and rule the city of sin.
Neither understood that the devil was in the details.
Neither lived to see the rising sun.

I'm Everett Ramses, son of Abraham, and I am the devil.

I took my rightful place as king of New Orleans.

Now, my realm is threatened by a man with false claims to the Boudreau family.

I know what I must have to secure my empire—*who* I must have.

The rightful daughter of Isaiah Boudreau, Emma North, must be my wife. Together we will reign stronger than ever before. But first, she must take the devil's deal.

*Have you been Aleatha'd?*

*From New York Times bestselling author Aleatha Romig comes a new romantic suspense duet set in the dark and mysterious world of New Orleans. DEVIL'S DEAL is a full-length novel in the Devil's Duet that began with the prequel *"Fate's Demand,"* continues in DEVIL'S DEAL and concludes in ANGEL'S PROMISE.

## ALEATHA'S NOTE TO READERS

The short story "Fate's Demand" is the prequel to *DEVIL'S DEAL*. It first appeared in *ONE MORE STEP*, a Bookworm Box anthology, entitled "The Deal." The Bookworm Book anthology was conceived with the concept that each author would receive the same first sentence. "One more step would mean certain death..."

"Fate's Demand" was recently released as a stand-alone short story everywhere for free.

If you haven't read "Fate's Demand," I recommend you download the free short story on all electronic platforms and read it first for background on our story. If you have read "Fate's Demand," you are welcome to jump ahead to the full-length novel, to more of Rett and Emma's story, *DEVIL'S DEAL*.

As always, thank you for reading and I hope you enjoy this dark romance.

*-Aleatha*

# Devil's Deal

By:

# ALEATHA ROMIG

# PROLOGUE

### The end of Fate's Demand

*W*ith a chaste kiss, one that left my own essence on my lips, Rett pushed the chair back to the table and returned to his seat.

My hands shook as I reached for my glass of wine. The red liquid quivered as I brought the glass to my lips. After consuming a generous portion, I stared beyond the candles to the man now casually dining upon his meal. A forkful of shrimp and an oyster on a cracker—it was as if we hadn't just...My head shook as I found my voice. "Let me get this straight. Ross made you a deal regarding me?"

"No."

"No?"

Rett dabbed the napkin at the corner of his lips, the same lips that had just brought me to ecstasy—twice.

"After both an in-depth conversation with your friend and my own diligent research, I contacted Mr. Underwood again and offered him a deal he couldn't refuse."

My head shook. "You can't make deals regarding people. It doesn't work like that."

Amusement again danced in his dark orbs. "My dear, the deal is done."

"Why do you think I'd go along with this?"

Lowering his fork to the plate before him, Rett sat taller and took a breath. "You are a marked woman."

I had to wonder if he was referring to what we'd just done.

Everett Ramses went on. "Your brother wants you dead."

I sat straighter. "Kyle died in the accident with our parents. He's been gone for over four years."

"No, my dear, Kyle O'Brien is very much alive. He's bided his time and now believes he can claim New Orleans. However, to achieve his goal, he must overcome two obstacles."

"Two?"

"Me," Rett said, leaning back in his throne-like chair and reaching for the arms, "and you."

"What do I have to do with any of this?"

"Kyle, your adoptive brother, is claiming that his stake to the city rests on the notion that he is the child Jezebel North gave up. You see, he's proclaiming that he is the true heir of Isaiah Boudreau."

The reality of Rett's words settled around me in a fog.

"My brother is alive and wants me dead?"

"He knows you're here, in New Orleans."

"What does that mean?"

"It means you will stay with me. I will protect you, and once you're legally Emma Ramses, you will be untouchable."

I stood, no longer able to sit still. Cool air flowed under my skirt, a reminder I was nude beneath.

"This is ludicrous. I should just go back to Pittsburgh."

"No," Rett said definitively. "I have had you under protection there since I first learned."

"There were people watching me?"

"That is done. Your home is in New Orleans."

My hands went out, coming back to slap my thighs. "And do what, Rett? My life is in Pittsburgh."

"Your education and dream is to be a writer. There is no better place in the world than here, but most importantly, you will be my wife." When I didn't respond, he went on, "I have men waiting to escort us away from this restaurant."

"Away, to where?" I asked.

"To my home. It's very safe."

My gaze darted to the door and back. "And if I say no? If I just leave?"

Rett gestured toward the door. "You won't, but as you are my future wife, I prefer not to hold you captive against your will." He shrugged. "I will, but I'd prefer you cooperate."

I tugged at my lip with my teeth as I contemplated all that had been said. "What will happen if I leave?"

"If you walk through that door alone, you will be vulnerable, not only to Kyle but also to his men. You may succeed in making it to the courtyard or possibly the sidewalk beyond; however, I can unequivocally say that...one more step would mean certain death."

## EMMA

*R*ett gestured toward the door through which I'd just threatened to leave. "You won't," he said, "but as you are my future wife, I prefer not to hold you captive against your will." He shrugged. "I will, but I'd prefer you cooperate."

The sound of Rett's deep voice rattled through my mind. His dark stare met mine even as my eyes closed. My pulse raced with the memories of what he'd done, what I'd allowed him to do to me. Lingering in a place between pleasure and pain, my core remained twisted with the understanding that in a matter of a few hours or less, I'd put aside all I'd known—all that I had heard with my own ears and seen with my own eyes—for the words, no, for the demand of a man who somehow scattered both my body and mind.

It was too much. I couldn't concentrate.

Much like driving on a dark night through a downpour, searching for an unknown street sign with the radio turned up, the driver reached for the volume and turned down the familiar song. It didn't lessen the falling rain, bring sunlight to the night sky, or make the sign more visible; it simply reduced the stimuli.

That was what I sought as Everett Ramses's demand lingered in the air, mixing with the concoction of the delicious aromas from the seafood smorgasbord, the remaining alcohol circulating through my bloodstream, and the dampness he'd facilitated between my thighs.

"Why should I believe you?" I asked.

"Because you know I'm right."

His response was simple and while ridiculous, there was a part of me, deep inside, that wondered if he could be right—*was* right.

Rett stood, pushing back the throne-like chair from where he'd made his decrees. My breathing hitched as with each stride he came closer. There was no need to rush; he knew his audience was captive, not as captive as I would be, but still, my high heels were rooted to the floor as I gripped the chair before me. The seams of his white shirt pulled with his deep breaths. His handsome face showed no signs of emotion.

The enticing cloud surrounding him added to the overwhelming assault on my mind. Wine, seafood, and rich, spicy cologne filled my senses as he pulled out my chair and encouraged me to sit.

"You see," he said as I sat and he stayed behind me. His slick timbre sliced through the air. "You know that what I've said is true."

Before I could speak, his large hands skirted up my arms.

They were the only part of him that I could see, yet I felt him behind me, his presence dominating my thoughts, settling the chaos as I concentrated only on him. Closing my eyes, I let his deep rumblings infiltrate my mind, setting off reactions within me; much like the silver ball within an old-fashioned pinball machine, they ricocheted from here to there.

The warmth of his touch moved higher.

"Think about it, Emma. The times you wondered if by chance you left your door unlocked. The sounds you heard in the middle of the night. The times you walked along a dark sidewalk, your senses on high alert as you looked left and then right, wondering if you were being watched. And the instances when you wondered if things were out of place, knowing they shouldn't be but having a feeling, one you couldn't shake."

Despite his warm touch, my skin cooled. With each of his phrases, I recalled an instance or maybe more. I was so lost in my thoughts that I hadn't realized where his hands had landed, what they were doing, until the pressure on my neck became uncomfortable.

"Your life has been in my hands, as it is now."

Alarm sent adrenaline through my circulation as I

reached up, tugging and prying at his fingers. Though my painted nails scratched, his grip didn't cease.

"You would be dead if it weren't for me."

*Was I to die tonight?*

He squeezed tighter. "Are you frightened?"

My lungs burned as I fought to fill them with air. I didn't or couldn't answer.

"Let it not be said, Emma, that I didn't give you a choice. Your choice is right here, right now. It's me or death." Rett's grip intensified as the pressure on my neck increased. His lips came close to my ear, warm air teasing my oversensitive skin. "I made myself a promise. If you chose death, it would be at my hands."

The panic that had been building within me evaporated into the humid New Orleans breeze blowing beyond the walls. Despite Rett's grasp, the dark spots dancing before my eyes, and the burning in my chest, I had a sudden realization, perhaps an epiphany. I dropped my hands to my lap, no longer fighting Rett's threat.

My reaction, or lack of one, had the response I'd expected—the response that I'd bet my life on.

Rett released my neck.

I couldn't help but gasp as air rushed into my lungs. It was similar to coming out of the water after diving into the deep end of the pool. As air filled me, my senses were turned up. Not only the aromas but everything—touch, sight, hearing, and taste.

The soft jazz music coming from the hidden

speakers was louder and the flickering candles were brighter. The world spun—not metaphorically but literally as Rett turned my chair toward him. With his tight grip now on the arms of the chair, he leaned forward until his dark stare was inches away from mine. With my complete attention, he questioned, "Are you submitting to death?"

"No." My voice was a bit scratchy. I tried to even out my breathing, confident in my next statement. "You won't hurt me."

The expression before me morphed as this handsome man took on a villainous grin. "Are you certain, Miss North?"

First, my name wasn't North. However, with each passing beat of my heart, I was certain of my statement. I was confident that if Everett Ramses wanted me dead, he wouldn't have pledged his protection even before I knew his name. If he wanted me dead, he could have very easily squeezed my last breath as his strong fingers crushed my neck, larynx, and trachea until I could no longer inhale.

I lifted my chin. "Yes, I'm certain."

Rett stood erect, his penetrating stare still on me. "You're wrong."

Reaching for the edge of the table and pushing the large chair back, I stood, keeping my gaze fixed on his. If this was a contest on who would blink first, I was giving it my best damn shot. "If I'm to believe you, Mr. Ramses, you have been protecting me from an unknown threat." I grinned. "Are you saying you're not to be believed?"

Almost imperceptibly to the eye, his head shook. Such a micro-reaction was the telltale sign that Everett Ramses was a man who rarely showed his hand. He kept his emotions and intentions close to the vest. And yet a moment before, despite his tenor and the level cadence of his words, he'd been pushed to his limit, showing me his true feelings. No, Everett Ramses didn't want me dead.

"Miss North, it isn't a lie when I say I could easily extinguish that glowing ember in your blue eyes. I'm a man of my word, and I meant what I said. You will be protected from your brother as well as other forces working against you." He lifted his chin. "With one exception."

"What would that be?"

"Not what, who." He inhaled, his nostrils flaring as he scanned me up and down. "Me, Emma. I won't make promises I can't keep. I won't pledge not to hurt you. I'm not an easy man. Marrying me will save you from your brother but not from me." Like lasers, his dark eyes scanned the neckline of my blouse. "You'll pay for my name and my protection.

"Pay?"

"With your loyalty and obedience. I told you before that obeying will bring you rewards."

He'd said orgasms, but I wasn't ready to interrupt him.

"Disobeying will result in punishment."

"Mr. Ramses, I'm not a child."

Rett seized my hand and tugged me forward until it was trapped between his grasp and his rock-hard erection, not so hidden beneath his expensive gray pants. "Do you feel what you do to me?"

My pulse increased. "Yes."

"I'm well aware that you're not a child, Emma. Children don't make me hard. I want a woman, a mature, sensual, and strong woman. Don't act like a child, and I won't treat you like one. Your job from this day forward is simple. Act like the woman capable of being my wife. Show the world that you were born to be the queen of New Orleans. As I said, that will make you untouchable to everyone except me." He pressed my hand harder against him. "I will touch you, Emma. Every inch of that soft skin will be mine for the taking. Just like my lips and tongue brought you pleasure, my cock will find pleasure inside you. I'll show you how a woman should be treated. With me, in my bed or wherever I choose, you'll find more pleasure than you knew possible."

With just his words, I was ready to combust, and after what had occurred earlier, I couldn't possibly argue the accuracy in his promise.

"But that doesn't mean I'll spare you pain. You, Emma North, will learn how to enjoy both." Releasing my hand, he continued, "Time is of the essence. Kyle's proximity is closer than I like. You asked what would happen if you left this room." His head shook. "I won't allow you to leave unaccompanied and end up in the hands of the man you considered your brother." He reached for my chin. "Listen to me."

This touch was different than seconds earlier. Everett Ramses may think he was a master at controlling his emotions, yet I saw the restraint in his expression. This touch was gentler, even sensual. The contrast from seconds before sent shock waves over my skin and through my circulation. It wasn't the wine that left me intoxicated as much as it was this man filled with mystery and a kaleidoscope of intense emotion.

"You're mine, Emma. Our union and marriage is what's best for New Orleans. It's also what is best for you; however, you should know that if the time comes when you change your mind and you choose death, it will be at my hands. What is your choice?"

*Who would willingly choose death?*

I lifted my palm to Rett's chest, splaying my fingers over the shirt. Beneath my touch, his heart beat a steady yet fast rhythm. For only a moment, I let myself gather strength. "Tonight, my choice is you, Everett Ramses." I tilted my head to the side. "I'm willing to see where fate leads. Just know, I'm not easily intimidated. Don't underestimate me. While I'm intrigued by you, I'm not a fragile flower you're saving from wilting. I can handle whatever you throw my way.

"However, you should know that just because you make me wet and are capable of providing my body pleasure doesn't mean you'll ever have my heart. I locked that away years ago. You decide, Mr. Ramses, is this still a deal you want?"

His arm wrapped around my waist, pulling my hips to his, his erection prodding my stomach as my neck craned upward. "I never offered love, Emma. This agreement is what fate demands of us both. It's a deal for my city and for your life. Love is a weakness, an Achilles' heel, so to speak. It's better that we both understand the limitations of our agreement from the start. My offer is for my name and my protection. Hearts are only useful to circulate oxygen through our bloodstream. Marry me and yours will keep beating. I have no other use for it."

Inhaling, I took in Rett's face. There was no question that he was handsome with his defined chin, his high cheekbones, and his protruding brow over his intensely dark eyes. The dark hair on his head was still mussed from where I'd woven my fingers through it as he brought me to ecstasy—twice. I found the man enticing and attractive.

*Did that mean he was a good man? A kind man? A man I could love?*

Those answers didn't matter. Love wasn't something that either of us sought.

Rett was asking for a commitment—a promise—to a legal agreement, one that I was certain would bring me pleasure in ways only this man could give. It wasn't as if he wanted my heart and soul. They weren't even mine to give. He'd never know why. It wasn't his business.

This agreement was to fulfill fate's demand. I could do that. A smile came to my lips. "I agree, for today."

"No, Emma, till death us do part."

# EMMA

*F*rom the moment I agreed to Rett's demand, our steps were a whirlwind filled with clandestine maneuvers. After leaving the room where we dined, we entered dark hallways. Unsure of my footing, I was steered by the steady direction of a large hand in the small of my back. With a change in pressure, I turned as Rett led us along tunneled corridors until he opened a door that led to a waiting SUV. The driver remained silent, only opening the door and allowing Rett and I to slide over the soft leather seat.

Once we were all within the vehicle, I watched as the driver nodded in the rearview mirror to Rett. Then, he slipped the SUV in and out of stop-and-go traffic as we made our way from the French Quarter to the Central Business District.

Despite recently learning that I'd been born in this city, New Orleans was new—to me.

The city wasn't new; it was older than our nation. Before the land was traded to the United States in the Louisiana Purchase of 1803, New Orleans was the territorial capital of French Louisiana. My love of history gave me knowledge of the past but did little to help me in the present. Old-fashioned streetlights gave way to tall office buildings as I tried to make out street signs or see landmarks that I'd only read about.

As we sat in the back seat of a moving SUV, I began to wonder if there was a parallel between recent events and this city. In 1803, the United States purchased the Louisiana territory for the ridiculous price of eighteen dollars a square mile. The legalities of the transaction could be questioned. History showed that the US paid France for property France didn't own, property, in fact, owned by Native Americans. My mind went back to the reason I was in New Orleans or the lie I'd been given.

I turned to Rett. "Tell me what deal you made with Ross."

Ross was my business partner and friend. The last term was used lightly. Nevertheless, Ross Underwood had convinced me to travel with him from where we both lived in Pittsburgh to New Orleans to meet with the mysterious investor, Everett Ramses. Somewhere between waking this morning in my apartment in Pittsburgh and earlier at the bar, a deal had been made —perhaps a purchase.

*Was Ross France and the Louisiana territory me?*

Before Rett could answer, the man in the front seat with one finger on an earbud spoke. "Sir, it's Noah."

Rett sat taller. "Tell me."

"He hit one of the targets."

Rett shook his head. "Only one?"

"Yes, sir. The others vanished."

Rett let out a long breath. "I want an ID. Get all the particulars and send backup for Noah before anyone unnecessarily stumbles across the scene."

With each bit of the conversation, my pulse ticked up a bit and my eyes opened wider, as if focusing my sight would help me understand.

Once the two men stopped talking, I turned to my side, taking in Rett's profile. I didn't pretend to know him, yet I saw the tight muscles in the side of his face and down his neck as his jaw clenched. "Rett, what's happening?" When he didn't answer, I reached toward him, laying my hand on his strong forearm. "Is this about me?"

Our tires went over a bump, causing all of us to bounce and my focus to change from Rett to the windshield. The city that had been outside the windows was gone, replaced by a dark tunnel illuminated only by long lights upon the walls that seemed to sense our presence, turning on as we approached and off once we were past. The way the SUV now pitched downward let me know we were headed underground.

"Tell me," I demanded.

Rett's large hand landed on mine as his lips thinned into a straight line. His head shook, once and only once, yet as the lights on the walls illuminated the inside of the SUV, I saw that his move was deliberate. In that moment, under his stare, as the small hairs on the back of my neck stood to attention, I had the sensation of a silent reprimand.

I spoke softer. "Please tell me what's happening."

His voice was hushed. "I have, Emma. Maybe you should listen."

Before I could respond, the SUV came to a stop. When I turned to look beyond the windows, a large gate was in the process of moving to the side, revealing a long cement staircase leading upward. "Where are we?"

"Your new home and you're here safely." As Rett spoke, a man appeared, descending the stairs. His black loafers and gray pants were the first to come into view. However, as he descended toward us, it wasn't his attire that caught my attention. It was both his size and his sheer bulk. With a bald head and visible gun holster, this man was the quintessential bodyguard. If there was a visual requirement for bodyguards, this man was their poster boy.

The driver opened the door at Rett's side.

Rett lifted his hand to me, palm up. "Come, Emma."

Placing my palm in his, I scooted until I was standing beside him. A cool breeze blew my skirt though I couldn't identify its origin. Sounds echoed throughout the parking garage, yet no matter what direction I turned, there wasn't anyone else present. The four of us were alone in a vast cement cavern.

"This is New Orleans," I said.

"It is."

"Is it safe to be underground?"

"This tunnel and garage are reinforced. When I say you're safe, I mean it."

Standing taller and lifting my chin, I asked, "Where are my things?" I hadn't seen my purse or phone since I'd left the table I was sharing with Ross. Back in my hotel room, I had a suitcase with a few items. There weren't many. My visit to New Orleans had been planned as only a two-day stay. When I left Pittsburgh this morning, I fully intended on returning to my home.

"Mr. Ramses," the large man in gray said.

"Ian." Rett turned to me and pulled something from his pocket. "Emma, you will have your things eventually. Trust me. You're safe."

Whatever he was holding had my attention. "What is that?"

Rett brought it up and let the material unfurl from his fingertips. "For your well-being."

I took a small step backward, my shoulders bumping against the car door. "What is that?" It was a rhetorical question. I recognized a blindfold.

Rett stepped closer, his voice a steady whisper. "There are things that you aren't ready to learn." His hands came to my shoulders, applying pressure and encouraging me to turn.

Instead, I remained steadfast as my head shook. "No, Rett. I don't want to be blindfolded."

With an exhale, he tipped my head forward and left a lingering kiss on my hair. "Humor me."

*Why?*

Why should I humor this man I didn't know?

"Because," he responded, answering my unspoken question, "this is the last thing I'll ask of you tonight." He lifted my chin until our gazes met. "Not because of my rule, Emma, but because you have entrusted me with your life."

"But why a blindfold? This is your house, right?"

"Sir, we..."

Rett raised his hand toward the driver, silencing the rest of the driver's sentence. "Emma."

Closing my eyes, I exhaled and turned, silently giving Rett access to place the blindfold over my eyes and secure it behind my head. Once he was done, he lifted my hand. "Go with Ian. He'll take you to your suite."

With my head held high, I nodded. Rett placed my hand on a sleeve.

"Miss North, watch your step."

Ian meant that figuratively since with the blindfold, I wasn't watching anything.

As we began to step up, I heard the closing of car doors before the SUV departed. While I couldn't see

Rett leave, I felt it. A strange connection between us had formed in a short period of time and with his departure, I felt as though there was a part of me missing.

"Miss North," my new bodyguard said, bringing my attention to him.

I sucked in a deep breath. "I'm Emma, Emma O'Brien."

"Please continue to step up. We're almost to the top."

"What is Mr. Ramses hiding from me?"

Making no attempt to answer my question, Ian continued his directions. "We're to the top. Now we're turning right."

Ian's directions continued through a labyrinth. With my vision obscured, my other senses kicked in stronger. Different textures of floors. We started on concrete, crossed hardwood, and now we were walking upon carpeting. Since leaving the concrete stairs, we'd climbed one staircase and then after walking, we went up another. The air around us was the steady cool temperature of air conditioning, and the only sounds I could distinguish were of our footsteps, Ian's directions, and our breathing.

He finally stopped. "Miss North, this is your suite."

## EMMA

*L*etting go of Ian's arm, I reached for the back of the blindfold.

"Miss North, please—"

I pulled on the tie, loosening the material as a large door before me opened inward.

"Please step inside," Ian said with a sigh as he reached inside the room and hit a switch.

Despite the lights, the room seemed dark, in need of an open window or doorway to the outside. Since it was nearly midnight, that would only add the artificial illumination of streetlights, but any additional lighting would help.

Before stepping in, I took a quick look to the left and right. The hallway extended one way with another closed door on the other side. The other way led to what appeared to be a landing for a staircase. The tall walls were covered in wood wainscoting with ornate trim to almost my height; above that was dark green. I lifted my chin, taking in the high ceiling and glowing sconces upon the walls.

"How will I find my way out of here?" I asked.

"That won't be necessary. The suite is well stocked. Beyond the main room are others: a bathroom, an exercise room, and a small office or sitting room." He tilted his head toward a large armoire. "There is a refrigerator in there with water and food for snacks. Your meals will be brought to you. There's no need to worry about getting lost."

As he spoke, my nerves from earlier returned, twisting and tightening with each phrase. I stilled outside the entry. "Wait, are you saying I'm supposed to stay in there?"

"Yes, Miss North. This is your suite. You're perfectly safe in here."

"No." I crossed my arms over my breasts. "I didn't agree to be a prisoner."

"I'm not privy to what you agreed to, ma'am. I get my orders from Mr. Ramses. If you have any problems with the arrangements, he's the one with whom you should discuss them."

Peering inside, I took in the heavy drapes over what I assumed were large windows. This was New Orleans. Weren't there usually balconies? It's two stories aboveground—a third-story suite—from what I could assess from all our walking. It was a long way, but maybe I could climb down if I needed to.

"Ma'am."

I let out a breath. "Tell Mr. Ramses I want to see him as soon as he returns."

"Yes, ma'am."

Seconds after I crossed the threshold, Ian began to pull the door shut. Before he could, I stepped in the way. "Ian, I had things at the hotel, and there's my phone and purse. I'd like to be able to contact Mr. Ramses myself." Not that I knew his number but still. "Will you please get me my things?"

The man nodded. "I believe you mentioned that to Mr. Ramses."

"Now I'm mentioning it to you, too."

"I'll inform Mr. Ramses."

It wasn't much, but it was something. "Thank you."

Before the door was fully shut, Ian's gray gaze met mine. "You are safe. No one will touch you here. You can rest knowing that."

With that the door closed.

Before I could take a step away to look around, the locking mechanism clicked, echoing in the otherwise silent room. My head began to shake from side to side as my hands trembled. Without taking in any more of the room, I turned, seizing the doorknob and twisting.

The fact that it didn't move wasn't a surprise. My overreaction to that realization was. Immediately, I balled my fingers to fists and began to pound on the solid twelve-foot door. "Ian," I yelled. "Ian."

It didn't take long before the lock clicked again and the doorknob moved.

"Miss North."

"Don't do that." Crossing my arms over my chest, I tried to regulate my breathing. "I don't like locked doors."

"Ma'am, I'll be right outside the door—or another guard will. Mr. Ramses wants—"

"He wants me to stay here, for now." I hoped the last part of the sentence was correct.

"Yes."

"I will. I won't even go onto the balcony...if there is one."

Ian's forehead furrowed. "The lock is to keep you safe."

"Who would break in to Mr. Ramses's home?" When Ian didn't answer, I went on. "And if someone did, would they get past you?" My new guard's lips came together in a straight line. "You may keep it shut, just don't lock it...please."

"Rest, Miss North. I'll be outside the door."

"The door will remain unlocked?"

Ian nodded.

I hadn't won the war. There was a guard stationed on the other side of the door with strict instructions not to allow me to leave; nevertheless, as the door closed and the lock wasn't engaged, it felt like maybe I'd won a battle.

Kicking off my high heels, I relished the plush

softness of the large rug that surrounded the large
canopy bed as I ran my hand over the heavy material of
the canopy. The floral rose pattern matched that of the
bedspread and drapes. Thick and luxurious, the fabric's
pattern reminded me of those seen in mansions of
yesteryear. The walls were white and textured, with
dark wooden trim. Even the ceiling was coffered with
ornate wood trim, creating multiple boxes at least
fourteen feet above.

The furniture appeared vintage. The posts upon the
canopy bed and the headboard were made of cherry,
heavy and solid. The armoire Ian had mentioned was
two-tone, reminding me of furniture my grandparents
had when I was young. Everything was clean and
spotless. I ran my hand over the top of the bedside
stand.

It wasn't as if this suite were forgotten and covered
in dust.

*Had my arrival been anticipated?*

Once I made my way around the main bedroom, I
stopped at the armoire, finding the small refrigerator I'd
been promised. Though I was no longer hungry, I
reached for a bottle of water, and twisted the top open.
The cap made the clicking sound.

After taking a long drink, I resumed my exploration.

Opening doors and flipping switches, I found all Ian
had mentioned. Beyond the large bedroom was an
exercise room. Though there were multiple pieces of
high-quality modern workout equipment and an open

space for yoga or exercising, the room was relatively small. I looked up at the large overhead fans.

The bathroom attached to the bedroom made up for the small exercise room. The surfaces glistened with marble tile and shiny faucets with sparkling handles. There was a large glass shower with multiple showerheads and a submerged tub big enough for two. Plush towels hung on the heated racks, and besides the mirror over the vanity, there was also a makeup table with extra lights. When I opened the drawers of the makeup table, I found a variety of cosmetics with brand names I recognized and others I'd only heard about.

That discovery led me back to the bedroom. While the drawers in the dressers were empty, the closet wasn't. It was sparsely filled. To one side was a robe and long satin nightgown. Feeling the soft fabric, I shook my head. This wasn't like any nightwear I usually wore. I was more of a boyshorts and camisole wearer. On the other racks were a few tops and a variety of skirts not unlike the one I was wearing, and various other items of casual wear. The shoe rack contained slippers, exercise shoes, and a pair of studded flip-flops.

A quick check verified that everything was my size.

My last place to search was what Ian called the office or sitting room. Opening the door, I was met with the aroma of leather and paper. Closing my eyes, I recognized them as the scents of a library, a place I loved as a child. My focus went to the floor-to-ceiling wooden built-in bookcase filling one wall. With fourteen-foot ceilings, there was even a sliding ladder much like Belle had in *Beauty and the Beast*.

With all that had happened, the familiarity of the books called to me.

I ran my fingertips over the spines as I read the titles of classics as well as contemporary women's literature, romance, and psychological thrillers. Many of the titles and authors I'd read, others I had on my TBR, and others were new to me. Pulling a familiar classic from the shelf, I opened the cover and inhaled the scent. There were two drapery-covered windows. Near one was a desk. Near the other window was an overstuffed chaise.

The large bathtub came to mind, but sometime over the last few minutes, a sweeping sense of fatigue had come over me. Reaching for a soft throw over the lounge chair, I curled my legs beneath me as I settled on the soft long chair. With it being nighttime and no sunlight trying to escape around the heavy drapes, I switched on a reading lamp, turned the page to the first chapter, and began to read.

*It was the best of times, it was the worst of times, it was the age of wisdom, it was the age of foolishness...*

# EMMA

*A*s I opened my eyes and the feel of soft sheets caressed my skin, I was met with darkness. For a second, I imagined I was home in my apartment in Pittsburgh. That second quickly faded as memories from an unbelievable night rushed back. It was as if a dam broke within me, drowning my thoughts in difficult-to-believe recollections. My heart beat faster; my breathing quickened. Blinking through the darkness, I recalled Everett Ramses, the reason I wasn't at my home. I saw his dark stare, recalled the sensation of his hands at my throat, his promise of death at his hands. My body battled as other sensations returned, how in an incredibly short time, he'd found a way to also bring me pleasure.

I remembered his solid chest, possessive touch, the way he captured my wrists as he'd seduced me in that dining room. I even recalled his rich, spicy cologne.

With a start, I sat up, suddenly conscious of the aroma. No longer contained to my memory, I inhaled deeper as I turned one direction and then the other in the pitch-black darkness. I lifted my own hand, unable to make it out as I blinked, willing my eyes to adjust.

The aroma came back, spicy and clean, wafting through the air.

"Rett," I called out.

*Was he present or were my memories that powerful?*

Once again, without sight, my other senses worked overtime. With the possibility that I wasn't alone, I was suddenly, uncomfortably aware of my nakedness beneath the covers. That led to the second thought: I was in bed, not in the sitting room with the big bookcase. My hands reached out, finding the sheets on either side of me were cool.

Pulling the sheet tightly over my breasts, I stared into the darkness, trying to make out what—if anything—was hidden in the shadows.

Was I imagining the scent of his cologne? After all, there were no other signs he was present.

Yet how did I get from the chair to the bed?

How was I undressed?

Even without more evidence, I sensed his presence. It was the opposite of what I'd felt as he drove away what I believed was last night. There was a connection we shared, one I couldn't discern. It was as his absence had created a void, and his presence was too overpowering to be hidden by darkness.

My pulse beat beneath my skin, thumping in my ears as I felt the sensation of him—his dark orbs upon me, peering through the darkness, seeing me, all of me, under the sheets.

I called his name again.

My focus went toward the windows. Knowing their location was purely from memory as there still wasn't light coming from around the edges. With my watch gone and phone still missing, my ability to judge time was limited. Yet it seemed as though I'd slept long enough for daylight to arrive.

Rett's deep tenor rippled through the darkness, bringing warmth even where there wasn't light. "The beauty awakes."

My breathing hitched as his words shattered the silence. I wouldn't pretend to know this man or even much about him, and still, I could sense his demeanor in the tone. It was closer to how it had been when we first met, friendlier if not even playful.

I liked it.

Closing my eyes, I saw the man I could only hear. I imagined his broad shoulders, wide chest, and possessive touch.

"She is awake, yes?"

"Yes," I said as I pulled the sheet closer and pressed my thighs together.

*How could a few words cause my blood to warm, my core to twist?*

"Rett?"

His response came nonverbally as the bed dipped. The scent of his cologne grew as I felt him move closer.

"Rett? Turn on the lights. What time is it? How did I get into bed?"

As my last question escaped, a finger came to my lips. "Do you always wake so inquisitive?"

Beneath his touch I smiled. "Only when I wake in a bed within a dark room, without clothes, and in the presence of a man I barely know."

"I carried you to the bed after finding you asleep in the library."

Library.

I leaned away from his touch. "And I didn't wake?"

"You spoke."

"I did?"

He found my hand and lifted it to his firm lips. "You asked me if I was safe."

*I had?*

"You said something about Charles Dickens."

That brought back my smile. "I was reading *A Tale of Two Cities*."

"Ian said you'd asked that I come to you when I returned." His warm breath tickled my skin as I made out his silhouette.

"I had, but I don't remember you being here," I admitted.

"You'd had a long day. I was beginning to wonder when you'd wake. It's after noon."

"It is?" I reached into the darkness, my fingers

splayed over his shirt. Beneath my touch, his heart beat in a steady yet fast rhythm. "It's after noon?" I tried to make sense of everything. "I never sleep this late."

His light touch caressed my cheek with a familiarity I wasn't certain we had accomplished. Such as with his tone, I would admit if only to myself that I liked it. My face inclined toward him.

"I've been watching you."

"Watching me sleep? In the dark?" A thought occurred to me. "Did you undress me?"

"I helped you. No one else sees what's mine."

The small hairs on my neck stood to attention. With my hand still against his chest, I strained to see him, his features. In the darkness they were there, hidden in shadows. "What happened last night?"

"I just told you. I found you asleep—"

"No," I interrupted. "Before that."

"You agreed to be mine."

That wasn't what I meant. "After you left. Where did you go? Were you in danger? Who is Noah and what or who was his target. What happened?"

Rett lifted my hand, the one from his chest, and curling my fingers, he molded it to his desired position. The warmth of his touch gave way to the firmness of his lips as he peppered my knuckles with kisses. "We discussed some of that last night. I have questions for you as well."

"I don't recall last night. Remind me," I replied.

"Tell me why you don't want the door locked."

My skin chilled. It wasn't a question I anticipated. "Ian told you."

"Emma, there's something you should know. In this house, in this city, there is nothing that I won't know. There are no secrets. Ian works for me and has been tasked with keeping you safe. When I'm not around, he'll sacrifice his life for yours. When I'm near, I will do the same. Now, tell me what happened last night. He said you seemed upset."

I was upset when the door was locked. While he'd just said there were no secrets, he wasn't being upfront with me either. My issue with locked doors was not his concern as long as the door remained unlocked. I pulled my hand away. "Maybe it was more than the lock."

"Talk to me."

I scooted back toward the headboard. "Gosh, Rett. Maybe I was upset about being bartered in a deal that was transacted about me while without me. Maybe I was a bit freaked out about being taken to an undisclosed location, blindfolded, and led to an abandoned suite. Maybe it's because I too like to know things and right now, I don't know or understand anything that's happening."

The warmth of Rett's body briefly covered me as he reached behind me, moving a pillow. "Lie back, Emma. I'll explain."

"Explain while I sit."

Rett inhaled. "Emma, my rules are simple. I've done

my homework on you." His hand came to my cheek, his fingers splaying and raking back through my long hair.

While his touch was gentle, I had a vision of the dining room and his hands around my neck.

"Not only are you stunningly beautiful," he went on, "you're also intelligent and creative. You have the ambition to accomplish whatever you put your mind to. I'm most certain you are capable of following my simple rule."

I teased my upper lip between my teeth, trying to recall. There was too much that had occurred. I wasn't confident in what rule he'd proclaimed. "Will you remind me?"

Rett tugged the sheet away from me, his cadence becoming more deliberate. "Lie down, Emma. Scoot down and rest your head."

Goose bumps covered my exposed flesh and my insides twisted as I complied. My blonde hair cascaded around my face as I settled back on the pillow, my mind swirling with possibilities of what was to come. Yes, I was naked; however, he'd undressed me and the room was still very dark.

"My one demand," he said, "is that as mine, you are ready for me, willing to obey whatever I ask, whenever I ask."

I remembered him saying that at the restaurant.

His touch moved lower. "Are you ready? Are you wet?"

My legs squeezed together. "I don't know you." It

wasn't an answer to his question as much as a statement of truth and uncertainty.

"You will."

I reached for his hand and held it tight. "Rett, I need answers."

"One question, Emma, and then I want to touch you as I wanted to when I helped you to bed."

"You didn't?"

"I prefer a fully consenting partner. Last night, I knew you were tired and saying things that seemed mixed up."

"Were you in danger last night?"

"Danger is everywhere—everywhere but here."

I released his hand as his proclamation settled over us. Despite not knowing where I was, in this place, he considered us safe.

# EMMA

*I* closed my eyes as Rett's touch roamed over my exposed skin. Maybe this was easier in the darkness. I couldn't see his expression or what he was doing. I relied on my other senses. As I did, it was as if Rett too was without sight. If he was, his actions would make more sense. With his light touch he was reading me, reading my body's story written in Braille. He began at my fingertips, gently kissing and sucking each one. His hands skirted over my arms, lifting them over my head.

Though he didn't speak or hold them in place, I knew he wanted them to remain there.

This position bared me to him as he traced behind my ear and down my neck. Goose bumps covered goose bumps as he peppered my collarbone with kisses until he moved lower. Though the aroma of freshness was around us, his cheeks bore a growth of beard that abraded my skin in the most perfect of ways. My breasts grew heavy with anticipation as his touch tweaked, his tongue licked, and his teeth nipped at my now-hard nipples. Involuntarily, my back arched as my whimpers echoed through the bedroom.

"Beautiful, Emma, close your eyes and get lost in my touch."

I was already there, a step ahead.

Painstakingly slowly, his kisses moved lower.

*Who was this man who could turn me into putty with his touch?*

I'd never been like this with anyone else, even men I knew and who knew me. It was as if Rett Ramses had an instruction manual on what exactly it took to turn me on.

"Open your legs."

I opened my eyes and brought my arms down, blocking his progress. "I'm not—"

A warm palm gently covered my cheek. "I know all about you, Emma. I don't care that you're not a virgin. I care that from now until your last breath, I will be the only one to touch you."

My virginity.

That hadn't been the end of my sentence. I pushed against his chest. "Rett, that isn't...what I meant to say is that I'm not ready for sex."

"You agreed to obey."

I nodded in the dark. "I know. I did and I will try.

What you did in that dining room was...I've never reacted...but I need to have some say."

Rett sat taller. I sensed his dark gaze on me. "Like the lock on the door?"

"Yes, like the lock."

"Lift your arms, Emma, as I had them, and spread your legs for me. I'll give you time if you continue to do as I say."

My heart ricocheted against my breastbone as I slowly lifted my arms. My pulse beat like a drum thumping in my ears. As my fingers searched the headboard, I wished for a brass bed frame or something to hold. The warmth of Rett's touch skirted over my stomach, reminding me of his second command. Without a reminder, I did as he'd said, scooting my feet up and allowing my knees to fall to the sides.

"I haven't yet touched your pussy. Tell me if you're wet."

"I am."

"Why, Emma?"

"I don't know. It's you and I'm not sure why I react to you like this."

"It's because we belong together. It was fate and neither of us can fight it. You were born to be mine. The gods knew what they were doing when you were created. As the daughter of a king, you're destined to be a princess about to be coronated a queen. And equally as significant, as the daughter of a whore, you're perfect to not only handle my desires but to also find pleasure in them."

*A king?*

*A whore?*

Before I could comprehend or respond, I let out a shout as two long fingers plunged deep inside me.

"Oh, yes, Emma. So responsive. Not only are you wet, you're tight." His fingers continued to work me, in and out, a third finger stretching me. "I'm not sure my cock will fit."

His free hand held me in place, splayed over my stomach as his other plunged and twisted. His fingers curled as he worked me into a frenzy. My mind couldn't think beyond his actions. Even his words were lost until he scooted down the bed and his warm breath blew upon my already-sensitive clit. With no other stimuli, I came, calling out his name.

It wasn't enough. Rett wasn't done. He buried his face at my core. As he had the night before, he licked and nipped, a ravenous man. The growth of hair on his cheeks continued to abrade my most sensitive areas as he held me captive to his ministrations.

The second orgasm came hard, nerve endings igniting from my head to my toes, as a fevered chill scurried over my skin. My thoughts were jumbled and my breathing labored as Rett moved back up my body, leaving a trail of kisses until our lips met. As his tongue sought entrance, I was lost to this man's ability to work me over like no one else.

No longer were my hands over my head but reaching out to his broad shoulders and weaving through his dark mane. As my touch skirted over his chest, I realized that while I was completely nude, Rett was fully dressed. "You're still dressed," I finally said as we pulled apart.

He didn't speak, but hummed his reply.

"You weren't planning on sex, were you?"

Rett teased a tendril of long hair away from my face. "As long as you keep up your side of this agreement, we have plenty of time for fucking. You, dear Emma, are a very rare and exceptionally fine wine. I don't need to gulp. I find immense satisfaction in sipping. For now, I want to savor having you here in my home where you're at my disposal day and night."

"I'm not a pet you can keep locked up to play with when you have time."

Rett sat taller. "You're not a pet. You're to be a queen. You won't be if you're dead."

"Is that another offer to take my life with your own hands?"

"No. It's a reminder that you're here for a reason. There's a war being waged."

*A war?*

I reached out and flattened my palm over his shirt. "What happened after you left last night? Tell me what danger is lurking."

"We'll talk. I suggest you go cover yourself. I'll have food brought up, and we can discuss things over lunch."

"Discuss things now."

His exhale filled the air. "When food arrives, I refuse to allow anyone to see you as you are right now."

"No one can see in this darkness."

"Listen, Emma. This isn't a topic for debate. From now until forever, I am the only one to see you nude and the only one to touch you."

While I wasn't complaining, I also wasn't sold that this was a forever deal. However, in the short time I'd had the rare opportunity to know Everett Ramses, I was keenly conscious that arguing that or any other point was...futile. I fumbled with the covers, freeing my feet. "I need lights to find the bathroom."

Rett got up from the bed before reaching for my hand. "Come, let me help you."

As I stood, he pulled me close. In that second, I knew that even if he hadn't planned on sex, his body was ready. Cool air surrounded me as he brushed his lips over my head.

"I won't wait forever. Sipping has its merits, but the more I have you close, the more I want of you."

It was a warning and a promise. I nodded against his shirt. Sex was going to happen. I couldn't even say I didn't want it. I could only say that I wasn't ready. The reason or reasons were getting more difficult to articulate. After all, Everett Ramses had brought me to ecstasy multiple times, seen me naked, and touched...well most of me.

I lifted my hand to his unshaved cheek. "Thank you, Rett, for waiting."

With each step, my muscles reminded me of Rett Ramses's talent when it came to inducing pleasure. Opening the door to the bathroom, Rett reached inside and hit the switch, flooding the room with light. My eyes squinted as I took in the sparkling marble.

It was as I made my way across the room that I heard Rett's voice. For a moment, my breathing stopped as I listened, assuming he was speaking on his phone.

"Go, we'll have our noon meal. Bring coffee too. Miss North did just wake."

"Yes, sir."

My chest contracted at the second man's voice.

*Was there someone else in the room?*

After all of Rett's talk of only him seeing me, had Ian or another man been inside watching?

Reaching for a towel, I wrapped it around me and opened the door. While the curtains were still drawn, the bedroom was now filled with artificial light. "Who were you talking to?"

Rett turned from the closing door. "Do you plan to eat our midday meal wearing a towel?"

"Rett, tell me who you were talking to."

"Ian. He'll bring the food from the kitchen."

"Was he..." My stomach twisted. "Was he in here?"

Rett's gaze narrowed. "No, Emma."

My gaze went to the door and back to Rett before I stepped back into the bathroom.

I tried to reason—it was simply my nerves playing tricks on me. The door wasn't closing to let him leave, but for Rett to speak to the man stationed there.

Still wearing the towel, I repeated that mantra as I took care of business, washed my face, combed my long hair, placed it in a messy bun with a hair tie I found in the drawer, and brushed my teeth. As I contemplated a shower, the door opened as if my privacy wasn't something Rett even considered.

Standing in all his clothed grandeur, Rett held the robe that I'd discovered in the closet last night. Now with the full light, his dark stare scanned me up and down. "Our food will be here in a few minutes." He held the robe toward me. "I'm having more clothes delivered. For now, this is better attire than a towel."

# EMMA

"Finish your meal," Rett said, nodding toward my plate.

After my interesting and erotic awakening, the midday meal we shared was the polar opposite. Tension bred from unfamiliarity settled around us, stealing our words and my appetite. More than once, one of us would begin to speak, only to stop when met with the other's stare. While I wasn't convinced I'd made the right decision in accepting what Rett claimed was fate, I had made a few observations. Based on the empirical evidence, I had no question that Rett and I could enjoy physical compatibility. My uncertainty hinged on the nagging concern that intimacy may be our only common ground.

As I pushed the food around my large bowl, I had the odd feeling that is associated with a blind date gone wrong or perhaps a misguided match from an online dating app. "Tell me something about you," I said in an effort to facilitate a conversation and perhaps to find shared interests.

Rett's dark stare met mine. "Emma, there are things you don't need to know."

I set my fork down beside the large bowl filled with green-leaf salad and slices of spicy grilled chicken. "You say we're to be married."

Rett nodded.

"Call me old-fashioned, but I'd like to know more about the man I'm to marry than his ability to bring me to orgasm."

By the way Rett choked as he reached for his glass of ice water, my directness may have caught him off guard.

One point for me.

Setting down his glass, Rett grinned. "On the contrary, my dear, by culture's definition of old-fashioned, sexual compatibility was never considered an issue. Women were expected to simply fulfill their wifely duties. It was all about the man's satisfaction in having his needs met."

"Then call me new-fashioned. I would like to know more." With me not having showered and wearing only the robe Rett had brought to the bathroom while he sat across from me, fresh with the exception of being unshaven, in blue jeans worn out in all the right places and a white button-down shirt with the cuffs rolled to below his elbows, the situation exemplified our current inequality. "Fine," I said, "I'll go first. What do you want to know about me?"

His cheeks rose as a grin came to his lips. "I told you that I've researched you all the way down to your preference of wine."

"There's more to a person than red or white wine." I sat taller. "For example, I enjoy the outdoors, hiking in the mountains, sitting near a lake, or on a beach." I stood, making my way to the window. "Speaking of which, it's too dark in here." I reached for the heavy draperies.

"Emma, sit and eat."

"After I open the curtains."

Rett stood, pushing back his chair. "Not..."

I pulled the cord. "What the hell?"

Beyond the panes of glass were barriers—solid, light-stopping barriers.

"They're shutters," Rett explained.

"Why?" I hurried to the other window and without pulling the cord, fumbled with the heavy drapery. Each window was the same; it was no wonder that sunlight hadn't shown around the edges. I secured the robe, and moving quickly, I entered the exercise room only to realize it was without windows.

I spun around, my fists going to my hips. "No."

Rett leaned against the doorjamb between the

library and bedroom with his arms crossed over his wide chest. The seams of his shirt pulled tight with each breath, and on his face was an expression I couldn't read.

"No," I repeated louder. "You're not holding me in a damn box."

Rett took a step toward me. "You asked me to be patient. I'm asking the same of you."

My blood pressure was rising. "So if I have sex with you, you'll let me see sunlight?"

"That wasn't my plan, but now that you mention it, there could be some merit to that."

"No." I pushed past him, going to one set of windows in the library and pulling the cord. The view beyond the panes was the same as the other windows. Fumbling with the old-fashioned latches, I found the windows opened inward. With the blue barrier now at my disposal, I searched. The shutter had no hinges, no latches, and no louvers. In my frustration, I pounded on the solid metal barrier. "No. I can't do this." No amount of pounding would lessen its hold.

Rett reached for my wrists. "Emma, stop."

I tugged to free my wrists, but I couldn't loosen his grip as he pulled them to my sides. "Let go of me." When Rett didn't move or reply, I pulled harder. "I've changed my mind. I'm not staying here. If I do, you're holding me against my will. It's a crime." My volume rose.

Rett's faux laughter echoed off the window panes.

"My dear, if you haven't figured it out yet, crime is what I do, and I do it well."

"You can't do *this*." I pulled against his hold.

"Calm down, Emma." His cadence was back to measured. "You're not being held a prisoner. You're under my protection."

"I'm calling bullshit on witness protection. I've watched movies and read books. You're not law enforcement."

"You're right, I'm not." He brought his nose near mine. Each sentence was punctuated with the scent of his vinaigrette dressing. "Listen to me. I'm going to let go of your wrists. When I do, you'll calmly go sit upon the chaise." Holding my wrists in one hand, he brought a finger to my lips. "I will not repeat my rule."

Apparently, doing as he said, when he said, was not limited to sex.

As I stared into his dark gaze, I wasn't certain what would happen if he repeated his rule. However, by the way the brown of his eyes swirled with black, reminding me of churning water at the bottom of a well, I decided now wasn't the time to learn. I nodded. "Fine, I'll sit."

Rett freed my wrists. I noticed that each one bore redness from his grasp. As I walked to the lounge chair, I rubbed one and then the other. Straightening my neck, I slowly made my way to the chair where I'd fallen asleep the night before.

Looking down, I saw the book I'd been reading lying on the floor. Adjusting the robe to ensure I was covered,

I sat perched on the edge. "There. I'm sitting. Are you happy?"

It didn't take a mind reader to know that happy was probably not Everett Ramses's top emotion at the moment.

"Are you?" he asked.

My gaze went to the open window that wasn't—it was blocked like the rest of them. "No, I'm not."

"You wanted to discuss last night."

While he hadn't stated it as a question, I nodded.

Rett reached into his jeans pocket and pulled out a phone. Pushing it my direction, he said, "Tell me who this man is."

After determining that this was how he wanted to proceed, I begrudgingly looked down at the screen. As soon as I did, I recoiled, turning away as the chicken salad I'd eaten churned within my stomach. "He's dead."

"I know he's dead, Emma. I also know the name on his ID. I want you to tell me who he is."

With my stomach ready to revolt, I again leaned toward the screen of his phone.

The person appeared to be a man, one with a hole or a void where part of his head should be. The lighting was dark, making colors difficult to distinguish, yet I was certain the glowing pool of liquid around his head was red and so was what was left of his dark hair. My head tilted. "I know him."

"Who is he?"

"I haven't seen him in years." I pushed the phone

away, my stomach doing more acrobatics as images of his brother, not him, tried to surface in the recesses of my mind. "I last saw him at the memorial for my family." My chin lowered to my chest as I recalled the memorial. I chose to have only one, a single service to celebrate the lives of my parents and Kyle. At the time, I hadn't been mentally or emotionally capable of three individual services. The funeral director recommended one joint celebration of life. And as I recalled the mourners, that dead man in Rett's picture had been present along with someone else.

"Emma."

I looked up, seeing Rett's clenched jaw and intense stare.

"Don't make me ask again."

I stood, meeting him chest to chest. Next, slowly and deliberately, I lifted my chin to meet his brown, almost black eyes. "He is...was," I corrected, "Greyson Ingalls. He was Kyle's best friend in high school. They roomed together their freshman year of college and both entered the same fraternity. They shared an apartment after graduation. Kyle died nearly a year later."

"And what do you know of Ingalls's whereabouts since you were led to believe Kyle died?"

My head shook as I took a step back. "You keep saying that, but Kyle did die. I know he did. I planned his funeral. I was there. I got the call about the accident."

"Mr. Ingalls?"

I shrugged as I wrapped my arms around myself, suddenly chilled. I'd known the Ingalls family for most of my life. Greyson had once been like a brother to me. I wouldn't let myself think about his older brother. "Nothing. I was in my senior year of college. They had lived in North Carolina. After their deaths, I moved permanently to Pittsburgh and didn't stay in contact with my or Kyle's friends from our hometown."

"Even on social media?"

"Remember what you said about having uneasy feelings?"

Rett nodded.

"I changed my social media to private and made a break from my past. Maybe it was survivor's remorse." I shrugged. "That's what the counselor at the University of Pittsburgh said. For whatever reason, I made the decision to make that break. It helped me start over by not constantly facing reminders of the life I lost."

"You're saying you've had no contact with Kyle's friends after that celebration of life—after you left North Carolina for good?"

I nodded and shrugged at the same time. The contact didn't directly involve Greyson, and it wasn't any of Rett's business.

"Is there more?" he asked.

"Nothing that matters."

Rett's gaze narrowed. "Now isn't the time to call out that lie, Emma, but just know that I know."

"What lie? I haven't...hadn't seen Greyson in over four years."

"That statement I believe." Rett turned and began to step toward the bedroom.

"Wait. Are you leaving?"

# EMMA

*W*hen Rett continued to walk away, I called out again, "Rett, wait." My command stilled his steps as he turned back my way. I hurried closer and reached for his arm. "Tell me why Greyson is dead. Tell me what the hell is going on."

Inhaling deeply, Rett spun in place until we were again eye to eye. "Fuck, Emma. I have told you. Your inability to either listen or comprehend seems to be a problem we will need to resolve."

I lifted my arms in the air and let them fall to my thighs. "What the hell are you saying? I am listening. I'm able to comprehend, but you aren't telling me shit."

Rett's chin rose. "Sit down, Emma."

Letting out a breath, I recalled his comment about treating me like a child and decided not to cross my arms and pout. Instead, I went back to the lounge chair and again sat on the edge. "Talk."

"Listen and listen closely. Do I have your attention?"

As I took Rett in, seeing and hearing his domineering presence encased in a toned and sexy body, I wanted to hate him. I wanted to demand my release and tell him that his theories of made-up danger were outrageous.

With each step of his jeans-clad long legs and the way his chest inflated with every inhalation, I questioned my presence in his home. And yet a small part of me believed I heard more than authority in his tone. There was also genuine concern. That element, whether imagined or real, was the component that kept me from running—well, that, the barricaded windows, and Ian on the other side of the door.

"Undivided," I replied.

"You are in danger," Rett began. "As I said last night, you're a marked woman. Kyle O'Brien, who now uses the name Isaiah Boudreau II, wants my city—New Orleans. He believes he can convince others, those who support my authority, that as Isaiah's son he is entitled to rule. His claim is nullified by your presence, by your being alive. If he can eliminate you, it will help to substantiate his claim as heir. That promise of future power is how he's enticing others to work against me. In short, he's orchestrating a coup."

"What will he or anyone else gain by taking over New Orleans?" I shrugged. "This isn't the Wild West or *Game of Thrones*."

"You're right, Emma. This is now and this is real life.

There is a de facto hierarchy that is constantly in flux around the world, one that most people choose to ignore. People assume that in a democracy they are participants in choosing their leaders. This isn't a political statement about those leaders but more about the masses.

"What I'm saying is that the people elected are figureheads, not the ones with the true power. That true power lies in dark allies and dimmed rooms.

"That power has been around since before our young country was a country, before Louisiana was a territory. What I'm talking about isn't limited to the United States. This hierarchy is present all around the globe. Those who reign don't come into that position by *we the people* or by votes. The ones who truly rule take their position by force and maintain their power with the same force.

"New Orleans became mine the night my father, Abraham Ramses, and your father, Isaiah Boudreau, decided they could no longer co-rule—no longer share what had been shared for generations. They both underestimated their true opponent."

"What happened?"

"They both succumbed to their injuries."

He had my attention. "Did you become who you are because you were Abraham's son?"

"My lineage helped, but as I just said, this position doesn't come easily; it must be earned."

"So if what you say is true," I said, "my father is

dead."

Rett nodded. "As is mine."

"You say that the Ramseses and Boudreaux ruled together?" My questions felt as if I were discussing fiction, not an alternative reality.

"They had. On that fateful night, Isaiah was left without an heir to fight for his position."

"Abraham had an heir—you."

"As I said, it takes more than blood in your veins to rule, Emma. I'd been preparing for that day—or should I say night—for a long time. The opponent my father and Isaiah underestimated wasn't the other; it was me. This city is now mine, and I won't allow the man now calling himself Isaiah Boudreau II to stake his claim as the king or co-ruler."

My head shook. "I still don't understand. Kyle's accident was over four years ago. Why does he want to kill me now? Why not kill me with our parents—if he's really alive?"

"I don't know."

My head tilted. "Really? *You* don't know? There's something the great and powerful Everett Ramses doesn't know?"

"I was made aware of this coup approximately eighteen months ago. In learning about Isaiah, a.k.a. Kyle, I learned about you. The O'Briens adopted both of you at the same time."

"Kyle was adopted too?"

Our mother would tell us that God had answered

her prayers with not one but two children, a boy and a girl. She never mentioned the fact that I was adopted. It was the tidbit I learned through the attorney after my family was gone. "I barely have any of the particulars on my adoption. Our parents never mentioned it. I had no reason to doubt that Oliver and Marcella O'Brien were our biological parents. After their deaths, the attorney gave me the records on my adoption but not on Kyle's. I didn't know he was also adopted until right now."

"The parents who raised you never told you or your brother that you were adopted?"

Swallowing the hurt that came the day the lawyer handed me the documentation and I read the truth, I shook my head. Standing again, I gestured toward Rett's phone. "Greyson is dead. Are you saying there's a connection to me? Does he work with Kyle?"

"We believe he did. Mr. Ingalls was at the restaurant last night—the same one where you sat with Mr. Underwood. Ingalls had been tipped off that you were in the city. Yes, Emma, you were his target."

My memories went back over time. "We got along— Greyson and I." It was true. "I mean all of Kyle's friends were a year older than I, and in their eyes, I was the annoying little sister."

A flicker of humor came to Rett's expression.

"What?"

"Nothing. I'm going to need more information. Whatever you can remember."

"I don't remember. I have spent the last four years

not remembering. I moved on and put that life behind me." I paced to the blocked window, the one that was no longer my main concern, and back. "Rett, it was difficult, agonizing, whatever adjective you want to use as a label. I'd lost my entire family only to learn that I wasn't biologically related to them. For my own sanity, I had to make the effort to move forward. My only other choice was to let the sorrow pull me down, and then, if I would have done that, I would have died right along with them."

When I turned, Rett was right in front of me. His large hands came gently to my shoulders. "Emma, you did that. You are a survivor. You're more than that. You were conceived and born to be a queen. I wouldn't ask you to do this, to recall everything you can, if I didn't believe that it was important. You have knowledge of Kyle that you've forgotten, information that could be vital to our cause.

"Your life is in danger. My city is threatened. Over the last eighteen months, my people have worked and infiltrated Isaiah's—I mean, Kyle's, men. What we know without a doubt is that for his plan to work, he must be the sole heir, which he isn't. You are. He needs you out of the picture."

"I don't understand why? I've never claimed to be Isaiah's daughter or Jezebel's." Rett's words from earlier came back, saying I was the daughter of a king and a whore. My chest felt heavy. "Is that why the shutters are closed so that no one can see me here?"

"The shutters work to keep what is within private."

I swallowed. "I can't live in a box, Rett. I want out of this suite, and I need sunlight."

Letting go of my shoulders, Rett went to the bookcase. I watched as he silently removed a book and turned it on its side as if to begin reading. When he opened the cover, I saw that what he held wasn't a book. It was a remote with buttons within.

Stepping closer, I asked, "What is that?"

"I was going to wait, but you've been helpful. I told you if you did as I asked, you'd be rewarded." He pushed a button and my face snapped up toward a new sound...and ceiling.

In the tall ceiling that I hadn't realized would move, a panel shifted to the side, revealing a large skylight now filled with blue sky and sunshine. Closing my eyes, I kept my face inclined, yet there was no warmth. The glass was tempered. And then there was a second sound and the glass moved. Warm, humid New Orleans air infiltrated the room as my cheeks warmed from the sun's rays.

Rett's hand moved around my waist until he had me pulled against him. "You are exquisite when you smile."

I hadn't realized my expression had changed.

My gaze met his. "I'm still in a box, Rett. This doesn't take that away." I looked up at the blue sky and back to him. "I'm also not ungrateful."

His large finger traced over my cheek. "Once you're safe and the city is secure, you'll have all the sunshine and freedom you deserve. I promised you your heart's desire." He tilted his head. "Tell me what that is?"

"My heart's desire?" I searched my heart and came up empty. "I don't know, Rett. I suppose I should have a long list of things such as wealth and possessions. I don't. I've always wanted to be a writer, and yet it's not the fame that I want as much as the opportunity to create something, anything, that can bring others peace and an escape." I shrugged. "I love to read, to get lost in words while those words paint pictures in my head. My mom..." I didn't correct myself as I took a staggered breath. "She used to tell me that there was no excuse for wallowing in self-pity. If I wasn't happy with my situation, I could transport myself to another place, another time. Whether that was as Elizabeth Bennet, Meg March, or anyone else, the choice was mine. I suppose in some way my heart's desire is to create a memorable world with a character who possesses qualities and lives a life that others would also enjoy inhabiting, if only for a while." I feigned a grin. "I know it's stupid."

"Desiring to create a world such as *Pride and Prejudice* or *Little Women* isn't stupid, Emma."

I was a bit shocked that Rett knew the characters I'd mentioned and the books they inhabited.

"It demonstrates your desire for greatness," he went on, "not for yourself but greatness in a way that helps others. I'll have a laptop brought to you. For now, it won't be connected to the internet, but you can write to your heart's content."

It was something.

"Thank you, Rett."

"Until that computer arrives, rest. A lot has happened. Besides the laptop, I'll have more clothes brought up. Spend the rest of the day relaxing and pamper yourself. Everything you need should be here. If it's not, there are papers and pens in the desk. Make a list of anything you need and give it to Ian."

Saying his name reminded me of earlier and my question of whether he was present when...

Before I could mention it, Rett went on. "Tonight when I come for you, I'll escort you to the courtyard and we'll dine under the stars." His thumb and finger lightly held my chin. "You're not my prisoner, Emma. You're now my fiancée, and my goal is to keep you safe until we can announce our intent to wed, to the city, the world, and your brother. With you at my side, no one will come against us. Together as a Ramses and a Boudreau, we will reunite the families and be unstoppable."

"I have..." I thought for a moment. "I *had* a life, Rett. I may not be in contact with those people from my childhood, but in Pittsburgh I have friends, people who will wonder where I've gone. And there's Ross. I know you made some kind of deal with him, but I should tell him I'm safe."

The ends of Rett's lips curled. "You are safe, Emma. I'm pleased to hear you say that."

"My things? My phone?"

"Patience. It's a quality we both must possess."

It seemed that in the search for patience, Rett held most of the cards.

With his last statement, he turned and walked away. I stood in the doorway between the sitting room and bedroom, leaning as he had earlier, and watched as he disappeared behind the main door. For nearly a minute, I waited.

The locks didn't engage.

That didn't mean I was less captive, but combined with the open skylight, it did make me smile.

# RETT

"*R*ichard Michelson is waiting for you downstairs," Ian said as I closed the door to Emma's suite behind me.

My eyebrows came together in confusion as I reached for my phone. There wasn't a message. "Why wasn't I informed? How long has he been here?"

"You said not to disturb you."

I shook my head. I had said that; however, there were certain exceptions. One of those would include a visit from one of the top prosecutors in Louisiana. "How long has he been here?"

"An hour. He's in your front office."

*Fuck.*

*An hour.*

I wouldn't wait an hour for anyone. The fact that Michelson had waited for me spoke to a few things: he was determined to see me and there must be a good reason. As a prosecutor, he could be a thorn in my side, but we had history that kept us allies. Nevertheless, finding a prosecutor in your home doesn't fill one with warm feelings.

*Had someone tipped him off about Ingalls?*

*Had one of my men been spotted before the scene could be cleaned?*

"Is he alone?" I asked.

"Yes, sir. He told Henri that perhaps he'd written the wrong time for the appointment and he'd be happy to wait."

"Appointment?" My gaze narrowed. "There was no fucking appointment."

Ian nodded. "Yes, sir, Henri and I know that."

Taking a deep breath, I turned and took one more look at the closed door before resuming eye contact with my trusted associate. "Emma is your responsibility, Ian. No one gets near her. I promised her a computer. Have one brought up, one without internet access. I'm also ready to have more clothes brought up."

"Wouldn't it be easier to move her to the other—?"

With the pressing of my lips together and slight shake of my head, I stopped Ian's question midsentence. Ian Knolls had been at my side since the night I took my father's and Isaiah Boudreau's lives. He'd been a significant member of my trusted circle before that night, helping me carry out the plan that landed New Orleans at my feet.

Over the years, Ian had been well compensated for

his fealty. He has had responsibilities that from the outside appeared grander and more significant than watching a door to a third-floor suite. The thing was that at this moment, nothing was more important than Emma North. Ian had been the one to oversee her surveillance in Pittsburgh when I couldn't. Keeping her safe here was less problematic and more imperative by the day.

I trusted Ian with my life; therefore, he was the man to trust with Emma's.

I responded to Ian's unfinished comment. "I'm not saying to bring up everything." I had a vision of Emma's magnificent blue eyes looking up at the sunlight. "She isn't ready for that. Have Miss Guidry help with the selection. Let her choose a few items she believes Emma will need for..." —I thought about a time period — "say, the next week. Include dresses for dining."

Ian's eyebrows came together. "Sir, it's your decision, but I have to ask. Do you plan to take her out of the house after what happened last night?"

Few people were given the luxury of questioning me. I was in charge. My decisions were mine for a reason. Ian was on the short list of people who I would answer. "No, I'm not talking about a stroll down Bourbon Street. I have a fucking mansion here that has sat mostly unused for too long." While I've kept it maintained, it has stayed quiet and unused since my mother passed away. "Tonight, Emma and I will dine in the courtyard. Maybe tomorrow will be in the grand dining hall." I kept my voice low. "The variety will give her something and someplace other than in that suite until the entire world is an option."

"There is another option to leaving her in there." Ian tilted his head toward the door. "The other..." This time he wisely didn't finish the sentence. Instead, he said, "Very well."

"No one but you enters her suite."

"I'll take care of it."

Taking a deep breath, I turned toward the staircase. With each step, my focus made the effort to shift from the beautiful woman I'd left behind to the business downstairs. It would be nice to say it was an easy transition, a flip of a switch and Emma North was forgotten and Richard Michelson's reason for a visit consumed my thoughts. However, as I set off on the most direct path to my front office, I wasn't thinking about the prosecutor.

As I descended the stairs taking me from the third floor to the second, my thoughts were filled with the woman I'd left upstairs. One look at the golden sconces and I saw Emma's golden hair. The light shining within reminded me of her smile as the sun beamed down on her cheeks. My footsteps down the hallway and the creaks of this old house disappeared as memories of her moans as I tasted her sweet essence came back.

In my lifetime, I'd had numerous successful

endeavors. From a young age, I found the most pleasure came before the acquisition. I enjoyed strategizing every possible outcome and planning for the hunt. There was a rush of adrenaline as the chase pursued, similar to that during a well-played game of chess. Plotting the demise of enemies and working to restructure the hierarchy of New Orleans dominated my thoughts as sleep was left at bay. No matter where I set my mind, I became obsessed with the preparation and details of the hunt and seizure.

In most cases, once a target was obtained, its value decreased and my attention waned.

Less than twenty-four hours of having Emma North under my roof, I found my fascination with her had increased, not decreased. Physically, she was mine. I told her she wasn't a captive, but technically, we both knew the truth.

While keeping her safe from outside forces, I'd facilitated the definition of captivity.

Emma North was mine.

Physically.

I would have her—all of her.

There wouldn't be a centimeter of her soft skin that I didn't touch. She would offer herself willingly to me as I pushed her to find pleasure in my desires. I had known that truth since I first learned of her existence.

Nothing about a physical relationship was up for debate. Even Emma knew that.

I had told her that there would be pain as well as

pleasure. I can only imagine what she thought I meant. While I had no issue with providing corporal punishment, that wasn't what I'd meant. The pain would come from within, her internal struggles and conflicts—battles Emma had before her.

That began today and it fascinated me. As I observed the moments when she battled with her own inner conflict, as her eyes swirled with uncertainty of whether she would comply with my one rule, I had the unusual realization that the hunt for Emma wasn't over.

Having her physically present was supposed to be enough.

It wasn't.

I wanted more.

When it came to ruling New Orleans, I continually redefined my goals to maintain my supremacy. That was what was happening, albeit unexpectedly, with Emma.

Now that I had her, what did I want?

*Obedience, submission, loyalty?*

*Would one be enough or did I need them all?*

*Was my list complete?*

The answer wasn't clear.

Maybe it was Emma's lineage that gave her the unique qualities I wanted to explore. Not only was she sexy and smart, but she was so fucking responsive. Damn, she came, her thighs squeezing my head, even before I'd taken my first sip of her juices.

There were stories...no legends, of Jezebel North's talents when it came to entertaining men.

*Was it possible that Jezebel had passed those affinities onto the daughter she bore and gave away?*

It was a nature versus nurture argument for another day.

I stilled for a moment at the top of the front staircase to the main level. As sunlight streamed through the stained-glass window behind me, I reminded myself that I was about to meet with one of my staunchest allies, and even so, I trusted very few. Nevertheless, entering the front office with my dick as hard as a rock wasn't the entrance I wanted to make.

"Thank you, Rett." I recalled Emma's sweet voice as the scene around me disappeared.

I didn't notice the sun casting colorful hues through the stained-glass window or the way those colors danced upon the red carpet centered on the dark wood stairs.

My head shook at the simple discovery. I could lay the heads of enemies at Emma's feet, overflow her jewelry box with the finest jewels, and fill her closets with the top designers, and she was grateful for sunshine.

How different would she have been if she'd been raised by Boudreau? If she'd been raised as the princess of a king? Would she be more like me, so familiar with the finer things in life that the wealth and opulence no longer registered and too consumed with victory to notice the warmth in a beam of sunlight?

Even though Boudreau and my father shared their

reign, it didn't much lessen their power or spoils of war. My home where I'd lived my entire life was an example of that grandeur. Nestled into the landscape of the Garden District, one of the most affluent boroughs, amongst the homes of lawyers, bankers, CEOs, and doctors, was the mansion owned by the kingpin of New Orleans. It had been that way for generations. I was the first Ramses to rule alone without a Boudreau.

Isaiah Boudreau's home had also been spectacular; however, it no longer existed.

Also located in the Garden District, the three-story mansion burned to the ground the night of his demise. Many said he started the fire himself, aware that his control had been taken away. Others said he ordered his butler to do it, unable to light the match to take his own life. Neither of those scenarios were what actually happened, but then again, this was New Orleans, the world where folklore was more often believed than the cold, hard truth.

My destination, my front office, wasn't where real work occurred; it was for show only. It was where people who requested an audience with me received it. In many ways, it was similar to the throne rooms of the British monarchy of old. Comparable to how peasants brought their petitions before the royals, that was the use of my front office.

Reaching the bottom of the grand staircase, I turned toward the double doors filling the arch that led to my throne room. I nodded at another of my men,

Henri. His duties included vetting anyone who wished entry as well as monitoring their presence.

"Mr. Ramses, Mr. Michelson said you had an appointment."

"We don't, but I appreciate his perseverance."

# RETT

S tanding outside my front office, I reiterated to Henri that there had never been an appointment scheduled with Richard Michelson.

"Yes, sir," Henri said. "I contacted Mr. Knolls when Michelson first arrived."

I owed neither Henri nor Richard Michelson an explanation of my delay. The simple singular thought of the beauty who'd been the cause would reroute my blood supply in a way I'd worked to quell.

When I nodded, Henri opened one of the tall double doors. With one exception, the room within had been decorated by my grandmother, my father's mother, nearly sixty years ago. The wood floor, twenty-foot ceiling complete with commissioned murals, intricate trim and crown molding, fifteen-foot windows, and shimmering chandelier never went out of style. If anything, in the world of modern minimalism, the ostentatious opulence spoke volumes.

"Everett," Richard Michelson said as he stood, vacating an antique velvet chair.

The use of my first name gave me the feel of fingernails upon a chalkboard. There were few individuals who had been granted that luxury of familiarity—this man wasn't one of them. It was a privilege he assumed had come with time, an assumption that due to history and his position wasn't necessary to correct.

"Prosecutor, to what do I owe this honor?" As I spoke, I gestured toward the chair where he'd been seated as I took a seat on the matching one. The room around us was filled with the bounties of my grandfather's spoils, gifts and bribes from around the world.

One exception was the fresh bouquet of lilies sitting upon an antique table separating me and Richard Michelson. That would be Miss Guidry's doing. At the moment, I appreciated even the minimal barrier.

We both sat.

Taking a breath, Michelson nodded and followed my lead to sit. "Today, I'm Richard," he leaned my direction. "I'm here as a friend."

Richard Michelson was a man small in stature. While his position made him powerful, there was nothing about his physical appearance that equated.

Closer to the age my father would have been, Michelson had gained mass in his midsection over the years, as well as graying of what hair remained.

The mental reference to my father was appropriate; the bond Michelson and I shared went back to him. There was a time long ago that Richard's daughter needed help that couldn't be found through legal means. My father not only solved the problem, but he also provided Miss Michelson with an opportunity that lifted her entire family financially as well as in status. Everyone, including Richard, was content with the outcome, with the exception of the problem. He ended up as alligator food in the Louisiana bayou.

Never underestimate the bonds created through crime.

"My man said we had an appointment," I said after we were both seated. "I'm most certain it wasn't on my calendar."

Richard took a breath as he gripped the arms of the chair. "Everett, I got wind of something that I thought you should know about."

He had my attention. "What's blowing in the wind these days?"

"We received a report of a possible missing person."

I shrugged.

*Wasn't everyone missing from time to time?*

"It's a woman, a visitor to the city. Her name is Emma O'Brien."

My attention was now focused.

"She checked into Drury Plaza yesterday afternoon," he went on. "There had been a mix-up with her reservation. While she was waiting for that to be resolved, one of the desk clerks heard your name mentioned. Miss O'Brien was talking to her business partner, Mr. Underwood. We assume that they weren't romantic—they had reservations for separate rooms. At some point, one of them mentioned a meeting with you."

I shook my head. "You'll need to be more specific, Richard. I am a busy man."

"Everett, I have to ask, did you have a meeting with an Emma O'Brien last night?"

"I had dinner in the French Quarter. You're welcome to speak to Elijah, the chef at Broussard's." Yes, Elijah was a trusted associate. I often used his private dining room for meetings of all natures—business and personal. He was extremely well compensated and knew to keep my information private. "My guest was a woman but not with the name of O'Brien."

"Who were you with?"

My cheeks rose as I curled my lips. "I have found it's better to not, as they say, kiss and tell."

"Is it because she's married?"

"Did you come here to discuss with whom I spend my cold nights? If that's the case, I believe you'll be bored to tears, Richard. Unlike you, I don't have a wife of nearly forty years who waits at home for my return."

He scoffed. "No, that's the description of bored to tears." He let out a deep breath. "Here's the thing, Everett: the woman's partner, Ross Underwood, was found this morning."

"Found?" This was news to me.

"Yes, in his hotel room. The COD is under investigation. There's evidence to suggest it was an overdose. What we can't determine is if that overdose was his own doing. There will be tests, but based on what was found at the scene, it looks like oxy. A quick check confirmed that Underwood had a legal script written by a doctor in Pittsburgh, where he lived. The question remains whether what occurred last night was self-inflicted or a homicide."

"I'm sorry," I said, "tell me what this has to do with me or his business partner."

"As I said, your name was mentioned. If only I had heard that information, we could keep it between us, but that isn't the case. The officer who did the interview is young. He didn't know. Now, it's part of an official report."

"I'll check my calendar, Richard. Sometimes people believe they have a meeting when they don't." Case in point, this assembly.

"Mr. Underwood isn't the missing person. Miss O'Brien never returned to the hotel. Her cell phone last pinged in the French Quarter." He leaned forward. "There's something else that has the NOPD scratching their heads."

I waited.

"Her hotel room was cleaned out—all of her personal belongings are gone—and there just happens to be missing recorded footage, ten minutes of deleted time on the hotel's security surveillance."

"That sounds like an inside job. Has the hotel staff been questioned?"

Richard nodded before his expression turned concerned. "This damn thing is blowing up. If we could just find Miss O'Brien..."

"Do you think this woman is in danger?"

"We believe there's a connection. She has a background in computers that might account for the hack in the Drury Plaza's security. Right now, if we're looking at a homicide, she's our number-one suspect."

I was a master at disguise, not in the way of illusion but in hiding my feelings, emotions, or reactions. It was a skill I'd perfected since childhood. I'd watched men die and not batted an eye. I'd even been the one to pull the trigger without any visible reaction, one that most would call normal. I'd listened as women professed their undying love or begged for pleasure, only to walk away.

And yet the prosecutor's last sentence almost was my undoing. "I'm sorry. Did you say that she is your number-one suspect? Then you're saying that she's dangerous?"

Richard Michelson stood. "Just do me a favor, Everett. I don't want you dragged into this. I'm trying to tamp down the flames. It has the potential of a front-page story that could burn down New Orleans again."

There were many tales of lore regarding multiple fires in New Orleans. While those were actual, what Michelson was discussing was metaphoric.

"Why is that?" I asked. "Not to sound callous, but people die in New Orleans every day." I had the picture of one man on my phone.

"I had a gut feeling about that name—O'Brien."

I shrugged. "Relatively common."

"It's an old story from when I was fresh out of law school and I was asked to help with something a bit unusual. I can't share the particulars, but let me just say that if this woman is who I think she is, she could be coming for you."

"For me?" I scoffed. "Are you suggesting that I should be fearful of a woman?"

"I've got a bad feeling." He shook his head. "There could be ghosts from the past coming back to New Orleans, and if I'm right, you would be in their sights."

*Their sights? Do modern-day ghosts carry guns?*

I supposed if he was talking about Kyle, the answer was yes.

Pushing off from the chair, I offered Michelson my hand. "Thank you, Richard, for the warning. I'll be sure to have this old house exorcised. No ghosts are welcome here."

He shifted his feet. "There's been some talk, and you and I both know that anything like this...anything that would put you into the spotlight isn't helpful. Your father saved my girl. I owe him to do the same. That's why I'm here, to warn you. Emma O'Brien could be a threat, maybe not physically, but her presence will start questions that are better left unasked."

# EMMA

"Tonight when I come for you."

It had been one of the last things Rett said before he left *my suite*, as Ian called it. Rett had told me to rest, and I supposed I should have listened. However, being in a cage, a box, or a suite, didn't facilitate my relaxation. With each passing minute, I found it more difficult to cope with this odd reality.

For a distraction, I'd decided to try the large bathtub. If I were to be honest, the bath was amazing. With multiple options for bath beads and oils, I was able to soak in the relaxing waters as eucalyptus filled the air and oils covered my skin in liquid satin. Once I was saturated to the point of pruniness, I climbed from the bath, stepped into the glass shower, and investigated the controls that looked more like an airplane's cockpit than a shower.

Water dumped from above, much like a spa, before

another showerhead rained over me allowing me to wash, rinse, and condition my hair. I confessed, if only to myself, that I was out of my league when it came to Everett Ramses.

There was a part of me that wanted to show him that I was capable of accepting anything he threw my way. That included the perception of my equality. If he were fresh and clean and dressed to perfection, I would be also. While there was something a bit erotic about the inequality during a physical encounter, I was determined that at all other times, I'd show him that I wasn't intimidated. I could be the queen at his side that fate demanded even if I wasn't certain what that would entail.

There was a lot I didn't know or understand. Instead of concentrating on the task he'd proposed as a whole, I found it helpful to break it into smaller, more conquerable chunks. As I showered, I concentrated on what the evening would bring.

*Would this be the night we consummated this relationship, or would the evening end with a handshake at the door?*

I refused to recognize that *the door* was the entrance to my place of captivity.

While I wasn't certain about consummation, I was confident that there would be more than a handshake. Despite the uneasiness during our midday meal, I found myself looking forward to—dare I say *excited for*—what the evening and night had to bring. In my mind, I began to build our impending dinner into more—into a date, for lack of a better term.

*After all, if two people were to wed, shouldn't dating precede the nuptials?*

My physical prepping and mental pep talk were interrupted by a knock on the door.

While Ian had the whole scary-bodyguard persona going for him, with each interaction, I found myself more and more comfortable in his presence. His knock came after I'd recently gotten out of the shower. I was wrapped in a towel with another towel upon my head.

At the sound of the rapping, I peeked from the bathroom door somewhat concerned that it was Rett and I wasn't prepared. "Come in," I called toward the door.

"Miss North." Ian stopped, wide-eyed, in the threshold upon spotting me peeking around the wooden door.

"I'm covered, Ian. You can come in."

He lifted a leather bag that reminded me of one I'd had in college but much nicer. "Miss, Mr. Ramses sent this for you. It's a laptop. Where do you want me to put it?"

"You can leave it there."

Ian glanced toward what remained of our lunch. "May I take this away?"

"Yes."

Before he left, he turned. "If you need anything..."

"I know, you're right outside."

"Yes, miss." His reply was accompanied by the first hint of a grin I'd seen upon his face.

The computer, blessedly, had a clock in the corner of the screen. I couldn't access the internet, which wasn't a surprise, but the clock was helpful. My only other indication was the sunshine from the skylight in the library.

I'd left that open.

It not only allowed the sunshine in but also the warm air.

I didn't mind.

While I was clean, I chose to be makeup free, my hair plaited into one long braid that rested upon my shoulder, until I knew more of what the night would bring. The jury was still out on what I would do or wear once I had more information.

Searching the closet again, I found a casual gauze skirt, lined in silk and different only in color from the one I'd worn the other day—this one was varying shades of navy blue—and a soft pink t-shirt. While I'd found a bra, my search of the closet and drawers came up empty for panties. I had a faint recollection of a comment at the restaurant when Rett had mentioned wanting me exposed. I was beginning to worry that he meant all of the time.

After I was dressed, another knock came. This time, I went to the door.

"Miss North."

It wasn't that I didn't want to be called by my real

name, but sometime during the last twenty-four hours, I'd given up on that particular battle. "Ian."

"May I enter?"

I took a step back as he came through the threshold, pulling a rack of clothes on wheels, one looking very similar to something that belonged in a store. The merchandise upon the hangers took my breath away until my breaths grew shallower as it became more difficult to inhale. "There are so many."

"These are only a few."

I ran my fingers over the material in all different textures and colors. "Do I need to look for my size?"

"No, I believe the shopper was given your measurements."

I turned to him. "When?"

"I don't know the particular date."

"Before today." It wasn't a question.

"Yes, the clothes have been arriving for a while."

For a while.

Rett has had this planned...for a while.

With each of Ian's answers and my subsequent revelations, my chest grew heavier. "I don't understand."

Ian forced a smile. "Mr. Ramses believes you deserve the best."

I looked again at the rack as I circled it one direction and then the other, my bare feet moving me forward. Finally, I asked, "How will I wear all of these?"

"I would assume, miss, one at a time."

A quick turn of my head and I saw that the man

without humor was trying to be humorous. While that was sweet, the clothes were overwhelming. "I mean, I won't be here that long..." —I turned to his gray eyes— "will I?"

"I'm sure that Mr. Ramses's intention was for you to have choices, not that you would wear every one of them."

Wringing my hands, I walked around the rack again, letting Ian's reasoning settle over me. "Yes, choices." I pulled one of the hangers from the rack. The style was simple—a halter top and an empire waist with a flowing skirt. When I held the dress up to me, the hem fell to just above my knees. "I like this one."

Ian nodded.

"You can take the rest away."

"But Mr. Ramses said—"

Hugging the dress to my chest, I forced a smile. "Please, Ian."

"Miss North."

I inhaled, feigning the strength and determination I was losing by the second. "I get the feeling you're supposed to protect me, keep me safe?"

"Yes, when Mr. Ramses isn't available."

My mind couldn't go to the question of my safety when Mr. Ramses was present. Instead, I forged ahead. "May I confess something to you?"

"I can't promise that I won't convey your message to Mr. Ramses."

"I understand that, and I appreciate your honesty.

It's all right if he knows." I needed to say aloud what I was thinking and feeling, a verbal affirmation that I was struggling. "I'm" —I shrugged— "overwhelmed. He said to rest, but resting gives me time to think, and thinking allows me to ponder what the hell is happening, and I appreciate the computer, but I'm not in a mind space to write a story, I can't even concentrate on reading, and if I would write, it would be the story I'm living right now, which is pretty unbelievable even for fiction, so instead, I'm taking in the sunshine, forcing the minutes to add up to hours, placing one foot in front of the other, and uttering one word in front of the other in a very long run-on sentence, and I can't" —I took a breath as I ran my fingers over the entire rack— "pretend to be okay with two weeks' or more worth of dresses. I can handle one dress for one night."

Ian nodded. "The blue one is lovely." He reached for the rack. "I'll take this away and bring it back" —he smiled— "tomorrow."

"Thank you, Ian."

He stilled. "There are shoes."

"More than one pair?"

"I'm afraid so."

Holding the dress, I sat on the edge of the bed.

"They're supposed to be your size," Ian went on. "Perhaps if you told me a color I could bring fewer choices."

Trying to regulate my breathing, I nodded. "I think we can work with that."

A few moments later, he returned with three pairs of nude high-heeled shoes in different styles with different heights of heels. I chose the pair in the middle. There was no good reason for that choice on my part. I didn't try them on or pretend to walk as if I were in a store. I simply reached forward and chose.

My current state of mental endurance was aided by lack of thinking.

As Ian started to walk away with the other two pairs, I stopped him.

"Yes?" he asked.

"Do you have any idea what time Mr. Ramses is coming for me?"

"He usually dines close to eight in the evening. If I hear any differently, I'll knock."

Exhaling, I looked down at the blue dress and shoes, and back to Ian. "Thank you."

"Yes, Miss North. I'm right outside."

As the door shut, I thought of how boring it must be to watch the outside of my door, the hallway, and the stairs. Even so, I didn't hate that Ian was there. I was in a strange house, an alternate universe, and yet I wasn't alone. I wasn't sure if it was the uncertainty or the warnings Rett told me about impending danger or everything in general. I couldn't deny that the things Rett said about his father and the Boudreaux had my nerves tied up in tangles. What I couldn't decide was if that was one knot or part of a larger cluster.

Going to the library, I looked at the computer

screen. Ian had said eight o'clock. My plan was to be ready at seven. In my strife for survival, I also decided to make short-term goals. Rett had promised dinner in a courtyard. I would be ready because even though I could see stars beyond the skylight, in a courtyard they wouldn't be confined to a rectangle. In that courtyard, I could experience the warm air, trees blowing in the breeze, and the allure of the outside.

# EMMA

*T*he sound of the door opening echoed from the main room. There hadn't been a knock as Ian had done throughout the day, but even from the library, I was confident of what I'd heard. The sound washed over me in a wave filled with both anxiety and relief.

*Was that possible for one action to do both?*

Anxiety was for the unknown. Relief caught me a bit by surprise.

*Had I feared Rett wouldn't come or he'd forget his promise to dine?*

Straightening my neck and shoulders, I scooted my feet away from the desk. The nude heels I wore clicked on the hardwood floor. Standing, I took one last look at the screen with the words and essence that I'd tried to compose.

The writing would wait.

Something told me that waiting wasn't one of Everett Ramses's strong suits.

I closed the laptop's screen and inhaled, causing the bodice of the blue dress to pull tight over my breasts. The style didn't allow for a bra, and I'd already discovered other underclothes weren't present. Smoothing the front of the dress, I glanced toward the window.

While it was still blocked by the shutters, in its current state, the glass had been transformed into a mirror. One quick look told me I was as ready as I would be. I was more prepared than I'd been when I was ambushed at the restaurant and also when I was awakened earlier in the day.

My makeup was appropriate for a night out, even if that only meant out of my suite. My long blonde hair was twisted behind my head. The humidity helped create the small curls dangling near my face and on my neck. I wore a pair of earrings Ian had delivered when he confirmed the time of Rett's arrival. Based on the size and despite the clarity, I assumed they were high-quality cubic zirconia.

Stepping to the doorway between the library and bedroom, my hand lingered on the doorjamb as Rett's dark eyes met mine, and my breath caught. Without thinking, my cheeks rose as I curled my painted lips. My expression wasn't brought on singularly by the sight of the man walking toward me, although I had to admit, Rett looked exceptionally handsome. The smile came because it appeared that I wasn't the only one who'd built this evening up to be a date.

It seemed that Rett had too.

He was no longer dressed in the blue jeans as he'd been earlier. Scanning from his combed-back dark hair to his leather shoes, I marveled at the sight of his clean-shaven cheeks, the definition of his chiseled jaw, and breadth of his wide shoulders. Rett's dark gray suit fit him to a tee. The jacket tapered in a V-shape, accentuating his toned torso. Beneath the jacket was a black shirt and a blue tie. It seemed that either Rett was in tune with the New Orleans spirits to predict the color of my dress, or more plausibly, Ian had passed on the information.

As I continued my scan down his gray pants and long legs, my lip slipped momentarily between my teeth as I entertained the fleeting memory of his erection prodding my stomach. In that second, warmth filled my cheeks.

As Rett neared, the rich, spicy aroma of his cologne mingled with the light, sweet scent of my perfume. My chin rose to keep my gaze on his as he came to a stop inches away. Taking a slight step back, he did as I had and scanned me from the tips of my shoes to the top of my twisted hair. Once the process was complete, his gaze lowered, momentarily settling upon the bodice.

When his dark brown eyes again found mine, he smiled. "You're stunning, Emma."

I'd received compliments from men in my life. The

father who raised me was generous with praises. Men I'd dated were also complimentary, and yet there was something about hearing those words from Rett that twisted my already-tangled insides. "Thank you. You're very handsome."

Turning slightly, Rett offered me his arm. "Join me for dinner."

It wasn't a question. He'd told me that he'd come for me. Nevertheless, the illusion of a date helped ease some of our earlier tension. "Yes, thank you." I placed my hand on his sleeve. With his hand covering mine, we stepped across the room.

As we approached the door, Rett slowed. "Before we go farther..." He reached into the pocket of his jacket, shattering the illusion as he showed me a blindfold.

No longer gleeful, I felt my skin chill. "Why?"

"Emma." Rett's deep tone reverberated through the bedroom as he pivoted, gently gripping my shoulders and turning me toward him. He tenderly placed his palms on each side of my face, cupping my cheeks and capturing me in his grasp while keeping my gaze on his. "I'm staring into the abyss. Your blue eyes have haunted me since you first looked my way last night. Truly, blue is an inadequate descriptor. They're so much more spectacular than in any photo I'd acquired. No camera can capture the magnificence of their depth. I'm not sure if you're aware, but your eyes tell a story. Through them, you speak without uttering a word. The shades change and sparkles ignite. As I look into the blue vastness, I see things I've never before imagined seeing with anyone. I see a beginning and a future."

When I began to speak, his finger moved to my lips.

"There's no limit to what I want your beautiful eyes to see, Emma. Sunrises and sunsets, snowcapped mountains and white sandy beaches, the wonders of this world and of the life we'll share. I'm a selfish man. I don't pretend it's not true. I want to watch as you marvel at all a life with me has in store. I want to be there as you learn and experience the future we can make together. The blindfold will help with that. It will do one other thing, something that I desire. Do you want to make my desires a reality as much as I want to make yours come true?"

I did.

Maybe I did.

I wasn't sure.

Speech escaped me as I floundered in the metaphoric cloud filled with the rhythm of Rett's timbre. His words and their meanings were less important than the way they were uttered. It was his cadence and tenor that had me enraptured. Embracing my newfound survival technique meant not thinking too far ahead...forging one step, one word, and one decision at a time.

"Do you?" he asked again as he released my face and placed the soft material in the palm of my hand.

I stared down. I realized that this wasn't the blindfold from the night before but instead one—

similar to Rett's tie—that matched my dress. When my chin rose, I was met with his expectant expression. "If I wear this, I'll be dependent upon you."

Rett nodded. "That's what I desire, for you to rely on me. I'm not saying you aren't capable, Emma. I'm saying you are. We both know that. Right this second, I see the conflict in your lovely eyes. There's a kaleidoscope turning with uncertainty as you wrestle with your own will. This decision isn't only about the blindfold. It's about you setting aside what you think you know, what you assume you've figured out, and all that you embrace, allowing me to lead you."

The thump of my pulse increased like drums, creating a rapid beat behind his voice. I didn't want to overthink this or any decision. It went against the plan I'd formulated.

Yet complying meant giving up my autonomy. I'd always been self-sufficient, but after the loss of my family, independence wasn't a choice. It was thrust upon me.

I did what I needed to do. I went on living.

My breasts pushed forward as I inhaled. "You're asking me to be someone I'm not?" I hadn't meant it as a question, but by the inflection of my voice, it was the way it came out.

Rett shook his head as a grin formed on his lips. "No, never. I'm not asking you to be someone else; I'm encouraging you to be who you were born to be. I've already confessed to you that I reign in a life of crime. I want you to take your place beside me, but first, Emma, you must learn to accept that there are things you don't know, things I do, and times when relying upon me is what will not only keep you safe but also bring you pleasures you never fathomed."

"Sexual," I said.

His smile widened. "Yes, but that's not what I'm talking about." He lifted my hand, the one holding the blindfold. "Let me put that on you, and then allow me to show you what I mean. This is a small sacrifice of sight for a short time. Do this and be rewarded." He reached for my other hand and brought my knuckles to his full lips. "You won't regret this." Soft kisses peppered my skin.

My survival technique was waning. Closing my eyes, I lowered my chin.

Rett's thumb and forefinger lifted it until we were again eye to eye. "Talk to me, Emma."

The last twenty-four hours had been too much for me to fabricate an answer filled with anything less than truth. "I'm afraid to trust you."

He stood taller. "Because of last night? You have to understand, I won't allow Kyle to be the one to take your life."

My head shook. "That's not what I mean, Rett." I inhaled. "I've found that since my family died, I'm safer —I don't mean from danger like you've spoken about. I mean my..." I almost said *heart*. "I'm less likely to be hurt if I don't give anyone else that much power. If I'm in control, I won't let myself down. I know I can depend on me. That's why I don't want to give up that power."

"I already have it."

My gaze went around the room where I'd been held and back to Rett.

Before I could respond, he added, "Taking power, money, status...it's what I do, Emma. I'm good at it. I'm not good at asking for it. If it helps, we're both on uncertain ground. I know from experience that there's no limit to what I can take. My desire is to learn if there's a limit to what you're willing to give, to sacrifice. This is me asking for what is already mine."

"I'm not yours."

"You are. You're mine to watch over, to keep safe, and to use however I please." He looked down at the blindfold and back. "At this moment, I'm not taking; I'm giving you the chance to show me that you trust me with that responsibility."

I peered once more at the blue material in my hand.

I'd taken the journey up to this suite blindfolded beside a man I had only just met. I could take the return journey with a man I knew a little better. Once again, our gazes met as I brought my shoulders back and lifted my chin. "Don't leave me or let me fall."

"Never, Emma. Not when you're at my side."

Exhaling, I handed him the blindfold and spun around as I'd done the night before.

After the blindfold was in place, with Rett still behind me, his lips came to my exposed neck and his

warm breath skirted over my skin. "Thank you, Emma."
A kiss and then another peppered my collarbone as
chills and goose bumps scurried over my skin.
"Submission given is sweeter than submission taken."

*Submission?*

I wasn't submissive nor did I want to be, and yet
Rett's gratitude, his warm breath, and his tender touch
created an intoxicating concoction that covered my
flesh in goose bumps and twisted my insides.

Rett reached again for my hand as he also wrapped
another arm around my waist. "Come, we'll dine."

Being tucked against his side gave me a sense of
security I hadn't had with Ian.

Similar to what I'd done the night before, Rett and I
traversed hallways and staircases. This time the
staircases led down. A slight change of pressure and
together we maneuvered long stretches of carpeted
hallways. When my footing was unsure, his grip
tightened. When I was more confident, he gave me
space. The interesting component of our journey was
that it all occurred without words. His guiding and my
following were as if we were in tune with one another,
and we moved in sync. The texture of the floor
coverings changed until he helped me down what I
would learn was the last step.

Without his explanation, I lifted my face to the
breeze, knowing we were now outside—in the
courtyard.

Rett's touch moved and I felt the tug on the material before it fell away.

Blinking away the sensation of the blindfold over my eyes, I sucked in a breath as I took in the miraculous surroundings. Slowly, I spun, making certain I didn't miss an inch of the world he'd brought me to. "Rett, this is simply magical."

# EMMA

*R*ett had promised me dining under the stars.

He delivered, thousands and thousands of stars, artificial in nature, white twinkling lights over our heads. The exterior walls of his home reached up to the dark sky in all four directions. There were multiple openings, solid doors and French doors that I assumed led to rooms within his home. With the lights inside turned off, it was only the courtyard that I saw.

My eyes widened with each discovery.

Even the trees were decorated in shining pinpoints of light.

In the center of the courtyard was a large fountain, one I'd guess was easily ten feet high. The water changed colors from pink to blue, to green, to red, and back to pink. Near the fountain was a table, one singular table with two chairs. The table was covered with a white linen tablecloth and in the center, as there had been at the restaurant, was a silver vase with a long-stemmed red rose. There were also two place settings complete with goblets filled with ice water.

It was as I spun around that I saw the maze of pebblestone paths lined with flowers. In the air, New Orleans blues wafted through the courtyard, its melody adding to our own private oasis.

"From the second floor," Rett said, "you can see that the paths form the Ramses family crest. The lights of the fountain illuminate the pebblestones. When all other lights are off, the crest changes color." He reached for my hand. "Before electricity, my great-grandfather mandated that the courtyard remain lit. Servants took shifts, assuring that the torches never extinguished. After the French Opera House burned in 1919, there were ordinances about the use of outdoor flames, even those contained. Refusing to allow the crest to go without illumination, my great-grandfather had this courtyard wired with electricity before the house."

I looked up at Rett with a smile as he spoke. It wasn't his story that brought me pleasure but the pride with which he articulated it.

"New Orleans," he went on, "was one of the first cities to have electricity, the Southwestern Brush Electric Light and Power Company, incorporated in 1881. However, getting that power to private residences took time. This home was one of the first private residences to secure its own electricity."

"Your family has lived in New Orleans for a long time."

"As has yours, Emma. The Boudreaux were here before the Louisiana Purchase. The history of your mother's lineage is less documented. The name North can be traced to many cities in Louisiana. The Norths are respectable in Baton Rouge. The rumor was that Jezebel was second-generation New Orleans. Her mother was brought down from Shreveport to pay a family debt."

"What does that mean?"

He lifted my hand and directed us toward the table. "It's a story, Emma. New Orleans is filled with tales."

"But how was she to pay a debt?" As the question left my lips, I knew the answer. "Are you talking an arranged marriage?"

"According to lore, she believed that was her destiny. However, upon her arrival, she learned it was less honorable."

I wanted to know more. "What happened to her, my...?"

"According to legend, she would be your grandmother, Jezebel's mother." He took a deep breath. "She was forced to work in a brothel."

"And her family was all right with that?"

"They didn't have a choice. Her work kept her father from reneging on his debt."

"And you said Jezebel was also a prostitute?"

Rett nodded. "Not the same."

"I don't understand."

He pulled back one of the chairs. "Please, Emma, I didn't plan on tonight being a history lesson."

I took the seat, sitting tall with my ankles crossed. Once Rett was seated across from me, I said, "You said this morning that I am the daughter of a king and a whore. I think I deserve to know more."

Rett's chin rose as he silently motioned to our side. Entering the courtyard pushing a wheeled cart was an older woman. Her clothes were simple, a dark blue skirt and blazer with comfortable shoes. As she came nearer, I noticed her white hair reflected the fountain's colorful lights. When she smiled, her hazel eyes sparkled, easing my nerves at meeting someone new.

"Miss Guidry," Rett said as he stood, "may I introduce Emma North. Emma, Miss Guidry."

Miss Guidry smiled as she clasped her hands at her chest. "My stars, you're really here."

I nodded, offering her my hand. "It's nice to meet you, Miss Guidry."

She clasped my hand between both of hers and squeezed. "The spirits be praised, Emma. You are just as I was told." She shook her head and looked quickly to Rett and back. "Now, I know Mr. Ramses doesn't like to hear this, but I have to say, your momma is real pleased you're home. She knows you'll do what she couldn't."

"Miss Guidry," Rett said, his tone sounding a bit like a reprimand.

Miss Guidry shook her head and waved her hand.

"Now, don't you never mind the musings of an old lady. I'm right happy to have you here. I'm getting too old to be the only one looking after Mr. Ramses."

"Miss Guidry," Rett explained, "has been taking care of this house since she arrived with my mother."

Arrived with his mother?

Miss Guidry winked my direction. "You see, I've been looking after him since he was knee high, well, before that." She lowered her voice. "He doesn't like me to remind him that I took care of him, should we say, back when everyone used cloth diapers."

I tilted my head forward as my fingers came to my lips, unsuccessfully hiding my giggle. I was most certain by the look in Rett's eyes that he wasn't a fan of any talk of his childhood, especially diapers.

"Now, now" —she waved her hand— "that was a long time ago, and these days all I do around here is keep this old relic together and oversee the cook and maids." She leaned my way. "Besides, I best believe you're more fit to take over the looking after of Mr. Ramses."

My eyes widened as I worked to contain my grin. "To look after Mr. Ramses? Well, that wasn't on the job description, but..." —I smiled at Rett and back at Miss Guidry— "from what little I've learned, I commend you. That task does seem like a job for two."

Miss Guidry let out a long breath. "I like you." She turned to Rett. "I like her. Now, be nice."

A giggle rolled from me as I reached for the glass of water on the table.

Rett grinned and bowed his head toward Miss Guidry. "*Nice*. I'll try to remember that." He raised his eyebrows. "Did you by chance bring our dinner?"

"Oh," she said as if she'd completely forgotten why she was standing with us. "Yes. Now, it's hot." Utilizing two black cloths, she lifted large silver domes off of the dishes on the cart and carefully laid them upon the table.

When she was done, I had a plate with grilled salmon, fresh green beans, and red potatoes, and another plate with salad and a roll. I looked back up at her. "Thank you. It smells delicious."

"Oh, honey. I don't cook. Never could." Her eyes widened. "But if you want to, I'm most certain Mrs. Bonoit would be happy to share her kitchen."

"Emma won't be cooking," Rett said.

"Wait," I interrupted. "I do like to cook. And I'd love to learn some recipes for New Orleans dishes."

Miss Guidry nodded. "I heard you were a good cook. Your momma said baking is what you really like. Well, Mr. Ramses isn't much for cakes, but he does enjoy beignets."

I was taken aback by her references to my mother, but she was right. I did enjoy baking. "I guess I'll need to learn how to make them."

Miss Guidry tapped Rett's shoulder. "I told you."

She nodded. "This right here" —she motioned between me and him— "is right."

"Thank you," he said, his lips straight, but there was a bit of merriment in his dark eyes. "I believe we'll eat now."

"Yes," she said, practically bouncing. "Now, just because Mr. Ramses doesn't eat desserts, Emma, don't let that stop you. I'll be back with some lemon cake."

"I'm not sure..."

Nodding, she backed away before realizing she'd forgotten the cart with the silver domes. "Now, never mind me. You enjoy your dinner."

I lifted my fork, and waited until she disappeared through the same French doors she'd used to enter. When I looked up, Rett was staring at me.

"I should apologize," he said.

My smile bloomed. "You're funny."

"I'm not sure anyone has ever told me that before."

"You ambushed me, practically kidnapped me" —I looked up toward the third floor— "have me held with a guard at my door, and the one thing you want to apologize for is a sweet old lady?"

"Miss Guidry isn't sweet."

"Yet you keep her around...since you were in diapers is the rumor I heard."

He shook his head. "She meant a lot to my mother. When Miss Guidry came here before I was born, the Ramseses became her family. I've offered her a home of her own and all the money she could ever spend, and she doesn't want it. When my mother passed, Miss Guidry said that her purpose was to watch over my mother and by extension, me." He widened his eyes. "I guess if you want to lay it on the line, I'm capable of many horrible things. The one thing I can't do is make her leave."

"Even with the offer of a home and money?"

He shook his head. "What sounds like heaven to one person is a hell for another."

My cheeks rose as I took a bite of the salmon. It was delicious, but that wasn't where my mind was. I was thinking that in that sweet old lady, I'd been given a glimpse into Everett Ramses. Under his tough shell, he might have a soft spot.

After finishing our dinner, we both enjoyed a cup of coffee and I had a small piece of the lemon cake. As I was finishing the last sip, I took a long look up at the lights. "Are there always this many lights out here?"

"No," he said, placing his coffee cup on the saucer. "I wanted to be sure you saw stars."

"You had them done today? For me?"

He pulled out his phone and smiled my way. "Close your eyes."

"What is your obsession with not allowing me to see?"

His eyebrows rose.

My eyes closed.

"Now open them."

It had only been a second, but in that sliver of time,

the thousands of lights overhead were extinguished. Now, the only light was the colorful display coming from the fountain.

"Look up and see your stars," he said.

I was again seeing the sky through a rectangle, but oh, this one was much larger than the one upstairs. The night sky was a velvet black sprinkled with stars. "It's so pretty."

When I turned back, Rett was standing and offering me his hand.

As I placed my smaller one in his palm, I confessed, "I don't want this to end."

"Nothing is ending. Once it's safe and you're my wife, this is all yours. You can spend as much time out here as you wish."

Less than a minute later, Rett secured the blindfold in place and led me back upstairs.

## RETT

Closing Emma's door, I scanned both directions and found only an empty hallway. A quick text to Ian and seconds later, I had his reply.

*"I'M SORRY, SIR. I ASSUMED YOU'D BE STAYING."*

Of course he did. It wasn't that I hadn't considered the possibility. Emma was fucking spectacular tonight. Before I arrived at her suite, I wasn't certain what I'd find. Would she be compliant and be ready to dine, or would she be defiant?

The incredibly intriguing discovery was that Emma was a little of both. I liked that. I enjoyed watching her inner struggle, the battle that raged behind her stunning blue eyes, igniting a fire that could keep me entertained for hours on end.

And fuck, her responsiveness was addicting. It wasn't even sexual, and yet she had my blood rerouting.

It began with the way she held onto me as we walked, turning when I turned, and working to be independent while willingly relying on my sight. That display was just a taste of what I imagined she'd be like in a more intimate situation.

And hell yes, many times, I'd imagined those possible situations. I already knew how incredibly sensual she was, the way her body tensed seconds before she orgasmed. The sounds she made as ecstasy overtook her and the flavor of her sweet essence.

Like the fine wine Emma was, the sample I'd tasted would never be enough. I thought a bottle would be sufficient, but now I believe I wanted the entire vineyard. I desired to take Emma completely and in every way. Like the calm of a lake's waters following a storm, I envisioned the satiation in her blue eyes after she was completely spent, her energy expelled, and she lay in my arms as our heartbeats found their natural rhythm.

It would happen.

I had no doubt.

Emma North was now mine.

I fought the urge to smile as I recalled her amusement as Miss Guidry rambled on. My heart beat faster as I envisioned her expression filled with wonder as she stared up at the stars. When she said she didn't want the evening to end, I understood; deep in my being, I shared her desire. It was a new phenomenon for me, one I wanted to explore.

Living my entire life in New Orleans made a man like me immune to the diversity of beliefs. Credit for my accomplishments didn't lie with unknown spirits or voodoo. I took what was presented. I held onto what I desired. If the world was a Cajun oyster, the fucking pearl was mine.

Never before had I put stock in fate. Nevertheless, as thoughts and images of the woman behind the door swirled with the intensity of a category-five hurricane in my mind, I mused that perhaps the demand fate had given to us was something beyond our collective understanding.

Heaven knew that I'd never been this entertained or interested or thoroughly fucking obsessed with a woman before.

What Emma and I shared, the known and unknown, wouldn't end.

Emma North was mine from today until forever.

I already held the power she admitted she feared to relinquish. The evidence was behind the door of her suite. Even if she wanted to leave, she couldn't. What she entertained now—what I allowed her to entertain— was the illusion of control. That was all it was, an appearance. Whether Emma joined me dressed in blue, red, or as naked as the day she was born was her doing. How she styled her hair and perfected her makeup was not my concern. Yes, she'd looked amazing, absolutely stunning, but again, these were inconsequential decisions.

The true power resided in her safety and now her legal concerns.

No, she wasn't aware that Ross Underwood was found dead or that the New Orleans Police Department, in all its infinite wisdom, had made her a suspect in Underwood's possible homicide. Perhaps it was selfish of me, but I didn't want her upset. My schedule was busy, our time together limited. I didn't want our time to be taken up with the news she could do nothing to change.

Bringing the screen of my phone to life, I sent a text to another of my top men, Leon Trahan. Much like Ian, Leon had been with me since I took over New Orleans, since my father's and Isaiah's demise.

*"MEET ME IN MY OFFICE IN FIFTEEN MINUTES."*

My phone immediately pinged.

*"WITH NOAH AT BROUSSARD'S. WILL BE THERE ASAP."*

I let out a long breath.

Noah and Leon were investigating the Underwood overdose. I was interested in hearing the updates. Regardless of what really happened, I knew the way I wanted the investigation to go. It was up to my men on the street, as well as those in the police department and even prosecutor's office, if necessary, to bring my plan to fruition.

At the sound of footsteps on the staircase, I looked

up from the phone. Ian's head appeared first, as he made it to the landing.

"Mr. Ramses—"

I lifted my hand. "I understand your assumption. Had it been correct, I would have appreciated the privacy. Don't leave her door. And for the near future, don't make any assumptions. I have no intention of spending the night up here."

"I...after this morning..."

"Keep Emma safe and remind her that she's being kept safe—a beautiful bird in a gilded cage is still in a cage. Remind her why." I recalled something Ian had said earlier. "Tell me again about the dresses."

"Miss North said she was overwhelmed. She only wanted one dress and one pair of shoes."

"Hmm. What about the earrings?"

"She said they were pretty, but that was it. I assume she wore them?"

"She did," I said, "Five grand hanging from each of her earlobes." I gave that some thought. "Either she is more accustomed to wealth than I realized or she didn't recognize their value."

"Do you want me to retrieve them?"

"No. Tomorrow, I'll have the diamond and ruby necklace for you to present." First, I must retrieve the heirloom from the safe. The necklace had been my mother's, commissioned from a famous jeweler in London. While my father had paid handsomely for it decades ago, the piece had only appreciated in value.

Tomorrow night, Emma would have ten grand on her ears and roughly three hundred thousand around her neck. I grinned as a fleeting thought of that being her only attire struck out of nowhere.

"I believe I know the necklace you're talking about."

"Yes, it will look stunning with a red dress." Or without. "Tomorrow, take her two dresses to choose from—both red." Illusion of choice. "And then present the necklace before I arrive."

Ian nodded. "Yes, sir. Did you tell her about Underwood?"

"No." The image of Emma's business partner deceased upon the hotel bathroom floor brought my mind back to matters at hand. Leon had procured a copy of the photo from the police report. I shook my head. "There's nothing she can do about it at this moment. If she knew she was a suspect, who knows how she'd react. It's better to keep her concerns focused on the here and now."

"I was speaking to Miss Guidry in the kitchen when you texted." Ian grinned as he shook his head. "According to her, the spirits are rejoicing. She is planning a large celebratory wedding."

While I was used to Miss Guidry's referencing spirits as her frequent communicators, I recalled how Emma's eyes grew wide each time Miss Guidry mentioned speaking to those who had gone on before us.

Ian went on, "According to Ruth, the deceased are already celebrating."

"She's right," I said, "about the marriage. It will happen." I took one last look at the large doors to her suite. "As for a large ceremony, time will tell. I'd be content with a private ceremony, one where Emma is well protected."

If I'd had any reservations about Emma's and my union—legal and physical—in the small amount of time I'd spent with Emma, they had disappeared. I was more than ready to have her as my wife, in my bed, and at my beck and call, but that wasn't the only issue at hand. First and foremost was her safety, quelling the threat posed by Isaiah Boudreau II. Second was this police matter, and third, her readiness to take on her role.

*Submission given was sweeter than submission taken.*

Emma would give it and we'd both find pleasure in that.

Nodding to Ian, I made my way down to the first floor and my real office.

My destination wasn't where I'd met Michelson earlier in the day. The summons I sent to Leon would bring him to my true inner sanctum. That was the suite of rooms where I conducted business, where life-and-death decisions were made and where destinies were decided. Few people were granted entrance to that suite of rooms and even fewer made it all the way within to my office. Entrance was given to the most trusted of my men, such as Ian, Noah, and Leon. Others made it farther than Michelson, and there were some who entered the suite and never left.

Technically, the shell of their body left, taken away to never be seen again.

I stepped through the threshold fully aware of the comfort I found within these walls.

# RETT

The inner office in my home soothed my senses like no other place could. There was the craftsmanship of the trim and paneling, the stately elegance of the furniture, as well as the lingering scent of expensive cigars and colorful spines of books filling shelf after shelf made of dark cherry. All of the elements added to the ambience.

This suite of offices had been constructed generations ago with the intention of both privacy and safety. While this inner room was without windows, it wasn't without character. The ceilings were fourteen feet high. The walls were twelve inches thick with two inches of metal welded into the center. Those within could weather a category-five hurricane or an attempted coup.

To enter the inner office required passing through

two other rooms. The door from the outside was camouflaged. The concept of hidden rooms and passageways was popular when this mansion was commissioned. Every entrance was also reinforced.

I took my seat in the worn leather throne-like chair at the large desk.

Inhaling, I ran my hands over the wooden arms, gripping the claw design at the end. It wasn't that I couldn't afford something newer, more stylish, and perhaps ergonomic. It was that my father, my grandfather, and great-grandfather before him sat in this chair. It was here that proclamations had been declared, summonses issued, and verdicts given.

Miss Guidry would say that their spirits resided here to guide me. I didn't believe that. I supposed that each man had set examples of ruling in this seat. I'd spent days and weeks in this chair reading through their handwritten notes and absorbing what they felt was worthy to be documented and saved for prosperity. Whether the examples were good or bad, I learned what to do and what not to do. I was granted insight into generations of New Orleans's important players.

The chair wasn't going anywhere and neither was I.

While the rooms had history, my great-grandfather, grandfather, or father would scarcely recognize the additions that we'd made in the recent past. Large computer screens dominated where long ago, reams of paper had been. In recent years, we'd also added technology to the mix of safety measures.

Nothing entered this room without my men's approval. Weapons were confiscated. Phones were prohibited. The only recording within these walls was done by us. No bug would pass our security. Our internet journeyed through layers of firewalls, bounced off multiple virtual networks, and was more classified than the federal government's, according to the government hackers on my payroll.

Some would say that I was paranoid.

That wasn't true.

By definition paranoid would mean that I had an irrational distrust of others.

My distrust wasn't irrational.

During my research of my forebears' journals, I was enlightened by the gift of time. I was in the future, knowing how each battle had ended and where mistakes were made. The world in which I ruled was one where my power came from overthrowing the one man who trusted me.

I wouldn't make that same mistake.

My distrust was rational.

A buzzer sounded.

The machinery could be likened to the antiquated equipment seen in *Mad Men*. The old relic was from before I was born, and I supposed I held a bit of sentiment for it. A quick tap of my keyboard brought my computer screen to life, adding modern-day surveillance to buzzers of old. I had the perfect view of the man waiting to enter and thermal imaging verified he was alone.

Pressing the button, I allowed the door to open.

Leon Trahan was what some would call a jack-of-all-trades; the man excelled in all he did. His long familial history in New Orleans and beyond gave him connections that weren't easy for outsiders to cultivate. His Creole heritage went back to before Louisiana was a state.

Leon and I met long before I was ready to take control of what was now mine. He was fifteen years my senior. Nevertheless, he helped me.

I helped him.

We found that together we could reach different people, achieve different goals, and that partnership made both of us incredibly wealthy. Leon also had connections—family in the world of criminal justice. It was a valuable resource for men such as us who worked the other side of the law. Leon had a brother within the New Orleans Police Department, a cousin who was a federal judge, and an uncle in a branch of the federal bureau that was hidden to most of the world.

If there was something to learn, Leon was the man.

If there was a plan that needed validation, Leon was my go-to.

"How is Noah?" I asked as Leon entered and the door behind him closed.

Small lines furrowed his brow, highlighted by his ebony skin tone. "He's busy. There was a problem at the tavern on Royal."

"I didn't hear about it."

"Nothing to hear. Noah took care of it. And in the process, he reminded a few of your tenants that late payments aren't acceptable."

"That shit never ends," I said, leaning back.

"No, boss, that revenue is too big to let it end." Leon grinned. "Best part is that there are people lined up to get prime property. If one tenant can't pay, we have ten to replace him."

As usual, Leon was right.

"Tell me," I said, "what you've learned about Underwood."

Leon's head shook. "There ain't no reason for him to kill himself. We've got a team going through the hotel security. Thing was, Underwood left the restaurant with his pocket full of cash as you instructed not long after Miss North accompanied you to Broussard's. We had a tail on him to see where he'd go with all that dough." Leon's lips made a straight line. "He ended up at Lafitte's."

Exhaling, I ran my hand down my face. "Fucking tourist."

Leon nodded. "Yeah, and he met a pretty little ginger there."

Ginger was Leon's term for a redhead.

"Working girl?"

"Don't think so. I ain't never seen her before. I'm not even sure she's from around here. She couldn't have been more than twenty-five. Hell, might be a college student. Underwood went with her to Place d'Armes. We hacked into their security and saw the two of them enter together around eleven. He left the hotel alone not long after two looking a little worn out." Leon smiled.

"I wonder if she helped herself to any of that cash."

"Funny you mention that. The police report didn't list the cash in the inventory."

My eyes widened. "Who is this ginger?"

"Well, according to the hotel registration, her name is Emily Oberyn."

Emily Oberyn was fucking close to Emma O'Brien.

"The clerk looked at her ID," Leon said, "when she checked in, but it's not hotel policy to make a copy. You know they do a lot of hourly business during the busy season."

I did know that. We increased their rent during those seasons too.

"Anyway," Leon went on, "Emily Oberyn paid cash and checked out at six a.m. The desk clerk on duty said Miss Oberyn had a car scheduled to take her to the airport. Noah caught up to the driver. He remembered her, said she tipped real well. He said he dropped her off at departures for United." Leon shook his head. "That's it. She fucking disappeared like the ghosts at Lafitte's."

"What do you mean?"

"We checked the manifests for all the United flights that went out yesterday, nothing."

"Are you suggesting she didn't leave New Orleans?" I asked.

"Boss, I got some people looking at the other airlines, but so far, nothing. We're hitting brick walls."

"Emily Oberyn is fucking close to Emma O'Brien. Maybe the police have them mixed up." When Leon didn't respond, I asked, "Could this Oberyn woman have poisoned Underwood?"

Pursing his lips together, Leon nodded. "It's possible."

"Even though he died later at the Drury Plaza?"

"Thing is, Underwood had a prescription—some shoulder injury from rugby. If somehow this woman knew that, she could have slipped him some extra oxy earlier in the night. I ain't saying it was enough to kill him, but then when he went back to his hotel, if he—"

"If he took his normal dosage," I said, interrupting.

Leon nodded.

"Why the fuck are the police suggesting Emma is the suspect? Why isn't the NOPD following this woman's trail?"

"I don't know why Michelson didn't tell you the connection or maybe he just didn't know."

"What?" I asked.

"Partial prints in Underwood's room likely belong to Miss North—Miss O'Brien."

My eyebrows came together. "What?"

"It would help if they could talk to her."

"No." I stood and leaned forward with my hands on my

desk. "Leon, this case needs to go away without involving Emma. Here's what I think. I don't know how her fingerprints got in his room." I planned to find out. "But the name of that woman is fucking beyond coincidental."

"Miss North ain't a ginger."

"But they're not investigating the ginger from what you've told me."

"No, they're looking at the scene. You know Lafitte's don't have video security."

"And neither does Place d'Armes," I said. "Fucking convenient."

"We only know about Lafitte's because you told us to tail him. He paid cash. They don't know he was there."

Clenching my teeth, I exhaled. "Here's the thing, Leon. I think that woman purposely had a name similar to Emma's. It was a trail the NOPD didn't find. Nevertheless, this was a setup to flush out Emma North. That isn't happening. The NOPD needs to rule Underwood's death as an accidental overdose or better yet, a suicide. Plant whatever you need to plant. Underwood lost funding for his editorial project. Bank foreclosed. I don't give a shit what tragedy he was dealt. When it comes to flushing out Emma, I smell Boudreau. He's not getting his hands on her."

Leon leaned back. "Boudreau is doing his fucking best to get under your skin. I see that. Here's what bothers me."

I took my seat again. Leon Trahan was one of the people who could offer his advice. "What bothers you?" A shit ton of things bothered me.

"The motherfucker came on the scene a little under two years ago, making his name known little by little. Then about six months later, he's making his claims to anyone who would listen."

That wasn't new information.

"Help me out, boss." Leon leaned forward in his chair. "Kyle O'Brien died with the O'Briens four years ago. Don't tell me Boudreau is some fucking Lazarus. Where the hell was he for two years?"

I stood and paced behind my desk. "It's the part we can't find. The missing fucking piece. Why would Kyle kill his parents, or arrange their death, and then disappear before making his claim?" I turned toward Leon. "Emma told me that the O'Briens never told her she was adopted. She found out after they died. It's not adding up. If what Emma said is also true for Kyle, how did he even know about the Boudreau name? How did he know the girl raised as his sister is a Boudreau? The city saw Jezebel with child once. He is claiming Emma's heritage."

"I ain't got no proof, but I got my gut."

A smile came to my lips. "Leon, I'd fucking trust your gut over a locker of evidence down at NOPD. What's your gut saying?"

"Isaiah Boudreau II is the pretty-boy mouthpiece

for someone else, someone who wants to bring you down."

"That list is fucking long."

"I say we start crossing people off, one way or the other," Leon proposed.

# EMMA

*a*s I followed my own plan—one minute, hour, and day at a time—it was as if I was living someone else's life. It was a life I didn't hate, but not one I would choose. In a nutshell, it wasn't my life, not as mine had ever been. While carrying on daily tasks, it was as if I were watching this other woman who looked like me, sounded like me, and even sometimes reasoned like me, but her actions were not mine.

*Is that Rett's goal...to change who I am?*

In a matter of a week, I'd fallen into a routine of sorts.

Other than the first day when I'd awakened to find Rett in the darkness, every other day, I'd awakened alone. It had been seven days since he'd brought me to ecstasy, since I'd asked for time to get to know him, and since he'd agreed. During those seven days, Everett Ramses was sexy and domineering as he pushed for things such as the use of the blindfold. In other ways he was a perfect gentleman, lavishing me with compliments, sending gifts of jewelry, holding my hand, and twisting my insides with kisses that would dampen my panties if I were wearing any.

Our interaction was limited to nearly a week of dining.

In the real world, I would never go on six consecutive dates in six nights, and yet now, it was becoming my obsession. Whether I'd willingly given Rett power or he'd taken it before I was fully aware of his doings, the inequality of our situation ate at my consciousness.

If I were to date someone six nights in a row, it would imply that I was asked daily, or perhaps nightly. I'd be left at my door with promises of a follow-up call. Or maybe I'd awaken to a teasing text, one that reminded me why I wanted to keep seeing the person.

None of that was happening.

Although I'd brought up the subject many times, I still didn't have my phone or internet. The other items from my hotel room had arrived. Other than the first day when Rett told me he'd return and we'd dine, each consecutive dinner was part of an assumption. Of course, that supposition was facilitated by the circumstances of my situation.

Each morning, one of my first orders of business was to open the ceiling.

I'd wake, open the ceiling, and then exercise.

Breakfast would arrive at 8:30 a.m. and lunch promptly at 1:00 p.m. Between the two meals I'd shower and dress for a day of staying exactly where I was. Either before or after lunch, Ian would bring in a dress or usually two. No longer did he wheel in the rack.

Many days, I spent with the ceiling open and a good book from the bookcase. Other days, or for a few hours on some days, I'd attempt to write, to compose a story that I was beginning to enjoy. I reasoned if I liked writing it, others may enjoy reading it. If I didn't, why should anyone else?

The story I was writing wasn't about my life. I didn't want to give my current situation that much validity. Instead, it was a story I'd made up based on nuggets of information from both Rett and Miss Guidry. It was the story of a woman brought to New Orleans, not as a whore, the lineage I'd been told was mine, but as the friend—a modern-day lady-in-waiting—to a bride. It was a story of adjustment, growth, and the importance of friendship.

*Did my friends wonder about me?*

*What did Ross think had happened?*

At six each evening, I'd stop my writing or reading and focus on preparing for our date.

A week had passed since Rett had given me thousands of stars. I never knew where we'd be when the blindfold was removed. Since the night in the courtyard, we'd dined in a stately dining room with a table that was set to seat twelve and could be extended to seat over twenty. Another night our meal was in a glass bubble, more accurately, a conservatory.

The conservatory took my breath away.

The nearly round room was completely made of windows. Even the ceiling was glass. While I wasn't sure where exactly we were in New Orleans, I was surprised that no other homes were visible. Beyond the room of windows was green lawn and tall flowering hedges. It succeeded in the illusion of isolation.

Truly, that wasn't an illusion any longer.

I was completely isolated.

I longed for connectivity to the world beyond these walls.

Whenever I mentioned my phone or internet, I was reminded to have patience and given the promise of *soon*. Patience was wearing thin and soon was never within reach. My only contacts were Ian, Rett, and occasionally, Miss Guidry.

With no internet, television, newspapers, or magazines, I had no knowledge of anything occurring outside of this suite or our dining location.

While I longed for some connection, physically I lacked for nothing. Anything I mentioned—be it yogurt for the small refrigerator or another throw for the reading lounge chair—it appeared within hours. Physically, my needs were met. It was emotionally that I was taking a hit.

With the one-week anniversary of my meeting Everett Ramses at hand, I finally understood what he'd said to me about power. He had it. I could dress up and appear his equal. We could converse about the editing program Ross and I created, or my life in Pittsburgh, or about Rett's family history and about the Boudreaux. I could choose to have dessert while he had none, and through it all, he had control.

In many ways the situation was similar to the first night with his fingers gripping my neck. Only now, it wasn't my throat and larynx he threatened; it was my emotional well-being. Rett said he wanted me to be his wife, but instead, he'd made me a dress-up doll kept locked away in a box that only Everett Ramses could open.

I battled with the idea that I was simply his distraction.

*Would I be brought out for a few hours or left to gather dust?*

In my unnerving situation, I hadn't realized the precarious position of my mental status or lack thereof until the sixth night, until last night.

Six o'clock came and I closed the book I'd been reading.

This one was a mystery set on the islands off the west coast of Florida. There were names of islands, towns, and even restaurants that I recalled from my childhood when the O'Briens would take Kyle and me for our annual family vacation to the Gulf of Mexico.

At seven thirty I was ready for Rett's arrival.

I'd worn a one-shouldered cream dress with floral lace

and a ruffled hem. The dress was fitted to show my curves, yet not too tight. To add color, I wore the necklace Ian had delivered nearly a week ago. It appeared to have diamonds and rubies. I emphasized *appeared* as I couldn't imagine the worth if they were genuine.

My shoes were cream with open toes and had a bit higher heel than some of the others I'd worn.

I'd left my hair down, curling the ends so that the large ringlets would cascade down my back. The red lipstick matched the necklace and the eye makeup was a bit more dramatic. Yes, I wanted his attention.

Eight o'clock came.

Eight thirty arrived.

The numbers changed with agonizing slowness, yet they continued to move.

At a quarter to nine, the doors rattled and my breathing stopped.

Yes, I was upset Rett was late, but the overwhelming emotion was relief that he'd arrived.

Until...

A knock on the solid door echoed through the suite.

My heart sank faster than the going down of the Titanic.

Disappointment overtook me as I dropped to the end of the bed. The knock came again.

In a week's time, Rett had never knocked, not once. He either appeared, as on the first day, or he simply entered. The knock meant one thing: Ian.

Refusing to acknowledge my level of frustration, I stood, pulled back my shoulders, straightened the skirt of the dress, and walked with my head held high to the door. Turning the knob, I pulled it inward. To avoid letting him see my shaking hands, I held tightly to the door. "Ian."

I wasn't confident in my ability to speak more without my voice giving away my distress.

"Miss North," Ian said with a feigned grin. "I'm sorry to inform you that Mr. Ramses was called away this evening. His errand is taking longer than he planned. He didn't want you to miss your meal." Ian stepped to the side, revealing a small cart similar to the one he used when he delivered breakfast and lunch. Upon the cart was one place setting.

Perhaps I should have questioned what took Rett away or if he was all right. At that moment, any questions were obscured by the massive disappointment growing within me.

*After all, why would the prisoner be concerned about the warden's well-being?*

"That's very thoughtful of him," I managed to say.

"May I?" Ian asked, gesturing within.

Inhaling, I made my decision. "That won't be necessary, Ian. Take it back to the kitchen."

"Miss, you need to eat."

"I have things in the refrigerator."

Small lines formed around his gray eyes. "Miss

Guidry added a lagniappe—an extra piece of lemon cake."

"Please be sure to tell her I said thank you. I would hate to be ungrateful for the food delivered to my cell." By Ian's change in expression, he took notice of my choice of words. "I'll pass." I took a step back. "Now, if you don't mind, I'll close the door."

Ian nodded. "I'll leave it here for a while in case you change your mind."

"No, Ian, I won't. And if I did, it wouldn't matter, would it?"

"Miss?"

Swallowing my emotions, I straightened my neck. "Good night."

"Good night."

I closed the door.

Stripping off the dress, I wadded the material and left it balled on the floor of the large closet. The earrings and necklace were left on the counter as I washed my face and went to bed for a night of restless sleep. Whenever I closed my eyes, I saw Everett Ramses.

At first the dreams were benign, dining and talking. However, as the night progressed, they took a turn. Rett's deep voice sent shivers down my spine. His rich, spicy cologne and warm breath teased my senses, and his large hands roamed my body.

"Emma, do you remember what I said the night we met what I wanted from you?"

The room around us was unfamiliar, yet I couldn't concentrate on anything besides the man dominating my senses. My lips closed, creating a straight line. He'd said so much.

Without another word, Rett stepped closer. We walked in sync until my shoulders collided with the wall and his firm chest pressed against my hardened nipples. His hand was in my hair, fisting it, tugging my head back, and exposing my neck. Kisses rained over my sensitive skin, their ferocity growing until they became nips and licks.

My breathing labored as I tried to keep up with the myriad of sensations this man could produce. His presence was everywhere at once, surrounding me, encapsulating me, and drowning me.

And yet there was nothing that he was doing that I didn't want. Maybe it was that I longed to be close to someone and in my current state of affairs, Everett Ramses was the only choice. Or maybe it was the passion in his touch, the possessiveness in his kisses, and the lust in his dark brown eyes.

"What do I want from you?" he asked, his hand still holding tightly to my hair.

I knew the answer, what he wanted. He wanted my submission, my willingness to be ready for him, day or night.

"I've never" —my voice came out heady and needy — "submitted to anyone, Rett."

"You want it, Emma. I see it in your beautiful eyes.

There's a storm brewing in there and you want to ride it out with me. I'm fucking hard as steel and you're wet, aren't you?"

I was. "I am."

"Submission given freely is what I need from you."

"I don't know how." It was my honest answer. "I want you too, Rett. I do. I want you to take me, but I don't know how to be what you want."

Releasing my hair, he took a step back as his dark stare scanned over the white dress. He ran his finger over the bare shoulder. "You do, Emma. You're doing it. You've been doing it."

I shook my head, knowing that I wasn't what Rett Ramses wanted. I was stronger than this. I survived tragedy by being strong. Submission was weakness. I couldn't be weak. Frustration and unmet desires brought tears to my eyes.

His command took me by surprise. "Lift your dress."

I could do this.

Once the material was balled up to my waist, Rett stepped back and scanned my exposed core. When our gazes met, his head tilted as he stepped closer and wiped a tear from my cheek. "Don't be scared. I'm looking at you, bare and exposed." He looked toward my breasts. "Your nipples are so hard they're tenting your dress." His finger came to my cheek. "This is submission, Emma. You're doing it."

"I don't know..." I didn't finish my sentence as Rett turned me around and unzipped the back of the dress.

"Let it fall." He eased it from my one shoulder. The material fluttered to the floor, pooling around the high heels. "Now turn back to me."

I did. The necklace felt heavy around my neck as I waited.

He reached for my chin and lifted it. "I want to see your eyes. I also want you to touch yourself, one hand in your pussy, the other on your breasts."

My breathing grew shallow as I did as he said.

I woke with a start to the dense darkness of the suite.

My hands were where they'd been in the dream as I stared out into the darkness.

"Rett?"

I wanted him to be there.

I didn't want him to be there.

Confusion clouded my reality as dreams and truth crashed, and I fumbled with the bedside lamp. Warm light flooded the space, erasing the shadows and my hopes that I wasn't alone.

The room around me was empty. I threw back the covers and quickly went from room to room, turning on lights and scanning the spaces I was beginning to recognize as mine.

Everything was as I'd left it.

Rett wasn't with me.

His presence, his encouragement, and his touch were only a dream.

"Damn you, Rett," I cursed as I lay back on the bed

and spread my legs. Disappointment was a bitch that I was unable to remedy. Sexual frustration, though, I had been there before. I could remedy that. Closing my eyes, I reached down, finding my own slick core. In the dream, he'd told me to touch myself.

This was my doing. "I will not be a doll left in a box. And I'm not submissive." My declaration floated in the air unheard by anyone but me.

If Rett wasn't going to get me off, I would.

My fingers found my clit, rubbing a rhythm until the tension rebuilt.

The orgasm was nothing to get excited about. Yes, it gave me satisfaction, but it didn't compare to what he could do or had done.

I wasn't going to think about that.

As I drifted off to sleep again, my only wish was that it hadn't been Rett behind my closed eyes as the unimpressive orgasm hit.

The next day, haunted by memories of a dream that wasn't real and dressed in a pair of soft slacks and a long off the shoulder t-shirt, I decided that it was time for me to start having some control.

I'd show him that Emma O'Brien wasn't going to bow to his wishes. I wasn't a doll in a box. The idea that occurred to me was only a small act of defiance, but it was something. Instead of waiting for Ian to knock, enter, and take away what remained of my midday meal, I would take it to him.

Pushing the cart, I stopped and opened the door. "Ian."

My eyes widened and my pulse beat in double time.

I stepped through the threshold.

My heartbeat echoed in my ears.

The hallway was empty.

I didn't take time to consider what I was doing. This wasn't small; this defiance went against everything Rett and Ian had said. It was also an opening, a path to freedom. I had to take it.

Quietly closing the cart in the suite and the door behind me, I took off toward the staircase.

# EMMA

*L*ooking down at my bare feet, I realized I hadn't taken the time to put on shoes or even socks. With my eyes wide open, I moved the direction I'd been taken each night, turning left from the door. A quick check over my shoulder confirmed that in the other direction, there was one door beyond mine on the other side of the hall. Beyond that, it dead-ended with a window, an unblocked window.

My fingers blanched as I gripped the square cap on top of the banister and took a step down. As soon as my weight pressed upon the stair, the wood creaked. I'd heard that sound before, when Rett was leading me. However, never before had it seemed as loud. My head quickly turned from side to side as I held my breath, waiting for someone to find me. The staircase was currently very simple in design, a polished oak with a smooth wooden handrail sandwiched between two tall walls. It paled in comparison to the other rooms in this house.

I'd assumed after the first night that the blindfold Rett asked me to wear was less about hiding the nuances of Rett's home than it was about me relinquishing my sight to him, allowing him to lead me, and trusting him. That said, I wasn't certain what I'd find once I was able to see more of his home. The dining room, conservatory, and courtyard had been magnificent.

Letting out my breath, I looked up. High above within the stairwell was a large intricate heavy metal light fixture as well as another unblocked window. Despite the landing and bend in the staircase, the natural light allowed me to see down to the next level.

By the time I made it to the second floor, my breathing was shallow. Too shallow. I stepped into the shadows past the landing and mentally scolded myself.

"Stop it, Emma. Breathe."

I peered around, recognizing that it was difficult to hear anything over my own thumping heart pounding in my ears. Wrapping my arms around my chest, I stood perfectly still and took in my surroundings.

There was a second set of stairs heading down to the first floor.

While I saw it, I was confident that I'd never been led down or up this second staircase. Peering again around the corner, I had memories of turning after descending the first set of stairs. Around the corner, I saw what I'd experienced without sight. There were high ceilings, luxuriously wainscoting-paneled walls, and a polished wood floor with a long predominantly red rug running down the center of the hallway. If the carpeting had been golden, it would be like Dorothy's yellow-brick road possibly taking me to see the wizard.

However, it wasn't yellow and the last person I wanted to see was the wizard, a.k.a. Everett Ramses. My goal was to find a way out of this maze. I didn't know where I was going or how to get there, but this was New Orleans. There were people and establishments. All I needed was the ability to make a phone call to Ross.

Now with a semblance of a plan at hand, I held myself against the wall and waited for my pulse to resume a normal beat. As I did, I tried to listen to the world around me. Faintly, I heard noises a floor below.

If my assumption was correct, this was a back staircase, perhaps one that had been constructed for use by servants. If I was right, going down the hallways would eventually lead me to the front staircase, the one I imagined to be much grander.

In my current state, I wasn't looking for grand. I was on the lookout for escape.

I took one step down and then another. As the staircase had done a floor above, this one came to a landing and changed directions. I held my breath as voices came into range. With limited practice and accessibility, I was still able to recognize both of them, quite the accomplishment considering I only could identify three people. Neither of the voices were of the man I was trying to avoid. That wasn't completely true. I was avoiding everyone.

The voices had been Ian and Miss Guidry. While I hadn't caught their entire conversation, their tones were jovial as Ian bid her so-long, for now.

Quickly, I hurried back up the stairs and turned the corner on the second floor. Pressing my body against the wall, I waited with my heart drumming against my breastbone as footsteps came closer. Closing my eyes, I held my breath. As long as Ian didn't stop on the second floor, I would be safe for now.

*Would he go into the suite and find me missing?*

If I'd thought ahead, I would have closed the bathroom door and turned on the shower. I hadn't given my escape that much consideration. Then again, if Ian simply kept an eye on the door, I had more time before he discovered I was missing.

Ian's footsteps continued upward.

I waited until Ian reached the third floor.

Once he did, I hurried back to the staircase and took one step down and then another. With another large window at the top of the landing, no matter where I moved, my shadow cast down the stairs to the floor below. I did my best to stay near the wall as I continued downward.

I was now low enough to see that beyond the stairs was a hallway.

I'd been right that this was the back or less-used staircase.

The familiar sounds of a washing machine and dryer came from a room to the left. To the right I saw two closed doors and straight ahead a kitchen. I could only see a small part, some cupboards and counter space. At the moment, I had no desire to see more or to learn if Miss Guidry was still there.

Holding tightly to the bottom square cap at the end of the banister, I took a quick check in the opposite direction, away from the kitchen and beside the stairs. My heart skipped a beat at what I found—a door.

A merciful, lovely tall wooden door with a large glass pane in the middle.

Beyond the glass I could make out concrete stairs and a sidewalk illuminated by the afternoon sun.

Holding my breath, I took one more look toward the kitchen and took off as fast as I could toward the door. I didn't have time to wonder if there would be an alarm or cameras. I just simply ran, coming to a halt as the old doorknob remained steadfast.

While continually checking behind me, I took notice of a small rack of keys attached to the wall beside the door and reached for all the keys. My body tensed as two fell to the old wood floor. For a moment, I stood perfectly still, waiting for my presence to be detected.

As time passed, I picked up the keys and held all five in the palm of my hand. My mind told me that opening the door couldn't really be this easy, but my beating heart said I had to try.

With a shaking hand, I inserted the first key. It went in, but wouldn't turn. The second key didn't even go into the keyhole and neither did the third. My surging circulation had me almost to the point of fainting when mercifully, the fourth key turned, the locking mechanism clicking as the dead bolt disengaged.

For only a second, I stood statuesque, waiting for the alarms.

My imagination ran wild with every movie I'd ever seen or book I'd ever read.

A pointed fence would descend and alarms would wail much like those found on a prison wall or those to warn of tornados. Hell, maybe even dogs would be released from their kennels where they were kept half-starved for just such a hunt.

The knob twisted as I pulled the door inward.

A welcome silence prevailed.

No iron gates.

No barking dogs.

No howling sirens.

Stepping outside, I quietly closed the door behind me.

Warm sun bathed my cheeks as I anticipated a New Orleans street filled with locals and tourists alike. Instead, I stilled at the bottom of the stairs, looking out over a concrete lot, surrounded by tall brick walls, complete with an ornamented iron fence sitting on top of the nine feet of brick.

My quick deduction was that this was where the Ramses estate or mansion or prison—I didn't have time to decide on the proper descriptor—received deliveries. Certainly, Everett Ramses didn't welcome guests to the kitchen and laundry room.

At the far side, in plain view of everyone, was a large iron gate.

From my distance, I wasn't sure if I could fit between the rungs.

There was always the possibility of climbing the bricks. But scaling walls had never been my forte.

It was then that I noticed a wooden door to the right.

Looking down and opening my palm, I stared at the five keys I'd appropriated.

Trying to avoid the wide open, I slithered along the wall as concrete bit the soles of my bare feet. When I finally made it to the door, I attempted to turn the knob. I couldn't recall which key worked on the house door to eliminate that one. Instead, I started over, one by one, and gave each key a try. I'd always heard that it was the last of *whatever* one tries. For example: I found my glasses in the last place I looked. Of course it was.

*Why would anyone keep trying after success?*

Once a key turned, the old hinges creaked as I pushed the door inward.

I blinked my eyes into the dim interior filled with the prevailing scent of must, followed by the scent of fuel. To the side was a workbench, complete with tools hanging on small pegs. To the left was an open space and a garage door.

With only one small window high above, I discovered that I was in a garage stall or maybe a gardener's shed. It wasn't the large garage I'd been taken to on the first night. This one was small as if it had been constructed before cars. Maybe a guardhouse or carriage house. I couldn't think of any other way to describe it.

The only door besides the one I'd entered was the garage door. One tug of the handle told me it was either too heavy or locked. I'd been about to give up when I startled at the sound of a motor.

A quick look up confirmed it was an electric garage door.

Quickly, I pulled closed the door leading to the concrete lot and ducked below a workbench. The sensation of spider webs sticking to my hair and skin made my flesh crawl as dirt and sharp grit poked at the soles of my feet. Holding my breath, I willed invisibility as the garage door lifted. Sunlight flooded the bay seconds before a large black SUV pulled inside and the huge door began to close. The windows were tinted, yet I could see a man in the front seat looking down at what I assumed was his phone.

This was my chance.

*Could I get out before the door closed completely? More important, could I escape before being noticed?*

I had images of a movie where heroes and heroines rolled to safety as large doors closed and dinosaurs came up inches short of securing their next meal. My only problem was that this wasn't a lost world and I wasn't trying to outrun a Tyrannosaurus rex.

The man I was trying to outrun was a much scarier monster.

One more look at the driver and I made a run for it, making it out before the door closed but not without activating the door's safety response. I was out on a hedge-sided sidewalk in a residential area with large palatial homes, and the big door was rising.

A quick dash and I ran beyond a large row of hedges. Afraid to open the gate, I waited, my nerves stretched to their limit.

*Did the driver see me?*

*Would he come after me?*

I closed my eyes.

# RETT

*I* tapped my pen on the top of my desk as Cole Kensington gave me some fucking excuse about what had gone down last night on the river walk. Cole was young, but he'd put in his time for me over the last few years, making his way up in the ranks by being street savvy and a quick thinker. The longer he talked, the more I believed I'd been sold a bill of goods. Other players had come and gone who made their way on looks, a smart tongue, and just enough knowledge and loyalty. I was over just enough. Either you were one hundred percent behind the Ramses name or you were one hundred percent against it.

I wasn't the only one listening to Cole's monologue. Noah Herbert was sitting to one side of him and Jaxon Cormier to the other. The whole incident last night had been a series of clusterfucks, and I was still pissed.

Kyle O'Brien, a.k.a. Isaiah Boudreau II, was continuing to be a thorn in my side, one that I was beyond ready to extricate. Despite my efforts, the man wanting my position and my city was disrupting the order of New Orleans. Last night a confrontation began as an altercation. Two men, fists flying—the fight was broken up by a street cop.

No report.

No consequences.

That was the first mistake.

NOPD was getting on my fucking nerves. I had a meeting scheduled for tomorrow with the police chief to discuss the way some issues were being handled and how that would change.

That fight wasn't two punks duking it out. No, it was the prelude to what was to come. A simple run of the men's rap sheets would have told the green-behind-the-ears flatfoot that the men involved were each members of rival gangs.

Two years ago, I'd settled the turf war for the greater New Orleans parishes.

I'd met with different leaders. They'd pleaded their cases and I listened. That's what a fucking leader did—listen. I also had men on the streets, eyes and ears. There had been enough rumblings.

When it came to last night's rival gangs, those rumors proved my instincts were right. The gangs had received an influx of green—cash—from dear ole Isaiah

Boudreau II in an attempt to turn them, not against one another, but against me. He promised a better New Orleans with him at the helm.

Last night, after the initial altercation, there was a meeting, one I should have fucking known about. By the time I got word, the minions were declaring war on one another and on me. They were courting Boudreau, claiming they could give him New Orleans.

There were times when a king sat on his throne and gave orders.

There were other times when the king's presence was needed on the street, in the fight, and fucking getting in my own shots. Last night was one of the nights that took me away from my throne.

With me on the scene, we quelled their siege. Shut it the fuck down.

The whole process, rounding up the men who would answer for the disruption, took longer than I fucking intended. Mostly because up until right before eight p.m. I had no intention of spending my night combing Port NOLA. Goddamned shipping containers made a maze complicated by Tetris—objects piled one on top of the other in a tight formation.

Leon, Noah, and I were on the street until after three this morning. We weren't alone. I had my troops out in force. As of now, one of the two gangs in question had new leadership, Jaxon Cormier, a tough kid with potential. The former leaders of both gangs were either gator bait or gator shit. I hadn't put that much time or research into the digestive process of an alligator when digesting two six-foot-plus motherfuckers who had pushed me too far.

One of the gangs with about twenty to twenty-five in number was served an eviction notice.

Get the fuck out of New Orleans and don't come back.

This realignment of hierarchy wasn't only for the two gangs or Jaxon. It was a message broadcast loud and clear to any leader or want-to-be leader in the parishes of greater New Orleans.

If it was discovered that you'd aligned yourself and your men with Isaiah Boudreau II, you would go down. If you didn't learn from the first reprimand, you were out of the city. Your turf was reassigned, and you were left without Ramses support.

As for Jaxon and the gang that received my endorsement, there would be a period of probation. He wasn't new to the area or the fight, just to leadership. Nevertheless, Jaxon came into power with my support and that of elders around the parishes. It took a fucking village or in this case, ten parishes or seventeen wards. When leaders weren't respected by other leaders, they became targets.

Every now and then, my gaze met the new young leader's. It was obvious that Jaxon was more than a bit unnerved by my command presence in my office. If things progressed as I planned, it would be a meeting he wouldn't soon forget.

I wouldn't tolerate insubordination.

Any contact with Boudreau needed to be reported to me; evidence of noncompliance would result in termination—not of the job but of life.

Last night it was discovered that Cole had received reports that hadn't been relayed to me. It was more than reports. Cole had been in personal contact with Boudreau and some of his top men. At this moment, Cole was doing his best to explain why Noah and I were left in the dark until fucking World War III had been declared.

As his statement became repetitive in nature, my mind began to wander. While I could think of better things, or a person, to fill my thoughts, it was time to declare this testimony complete.

Court was to be adjourned by the judge and jury—me.

Cole Kensington had been flapping his gums for nearly forty-five minutes, and that was three quarters of an hour longer than I cared to listen. The phone in my pocket vibrated as my computer dinged. My eye twitched with displeasure. I'd given strict do-not-disturb orders; someone would be read the riot act.

Between not seeing Emma last night and a maximum of three hours' sleep, any patience I'd previously held was not only worn, it was gone.

Pushing off from the edge of my desk, my chair

moved backward, and I stood. My movement silenced Mr. Cole Kensington. His complexion paled as silence prevailed.

"When were you first contacted by Isaiah Boudreau II?" I asked.

Perspiration glistened on Cole's brow as he swallowed and readjusted his footing. "Boss, I'm not sure of the first time."

"Yesterday?" Noah asked.

"A week ago," I offered.

"It was...well, at first I didn't believe it was him. I mean," Cole rambled, "it ain't like I knew what he looked like. I first met his friend, some guy named Ingalls. He and his brother were taking bets."

Greyson Ingalls was no longer alive. His brother William, a year older, still was. Both had a history that included Kyle O'Brien. With William, his history wasn't limited to Kyle. That was the matter I mentioned to Emma that one day we'd revisit.

"Bets in my city?" I asked.

Cole nodded. "Yeah, that's why I was checking it out. While I was watching what was going down, this guy came up, real casual like, in Fahy's and started talking." Cole shook his head. "He didn't say his name, just some friend of the Ingalls brothers." His words and phrases came faster. "The next time I saw him, he challenged me to a game of pool."

Fahy's was a hole-in-the-wall on the outskirts of the French Quarter, a local hangout with delicious jambalaya and an array of illegal slots. It sounded like there was also some under-the-table betting going on. The only part of Cole's story I believed involved pool. There were two tables back by the slots.

Noah stood. "When was this, Cole?"

"About two months ago."

"Two months?" I asked.

Cole shook his head. "I think it was three. Yeah. Three."

Jaxon remained silent, watching each speaker as if he was watching a tennis match.

"Do we pay you enough?" I asked.

"Why, yes, Mr. Ramses." His head bobbed.

"Enough to buy yourself an expensive Jag?"

Cole's eyes opened wide. "No. It ain't like that. You see...my cousin, the one in Baton Rouge, yeah, his name is Kevin, and he got himself in with a loan shark and well, Kevin has a few problems. He's always short. My cousin asked me to buy that car for cheap. Cash. Practically nothing. He didn't want the moneylender to take it."

I took a deep breath. "Thank you, Mr. Kensington, for meeting with us today."

"Yes, sir, Mr. Ramses. I want you to know I have your back." He turned to Jaxon. "And I'm here for you. Got any questions, just ask, man."

My phone vibrated again.

Fucking day wouldn't end.

"Did Mr. Boudreau give you any contact information?" Noah asked.

"No."

Cole's answer came too fast. Per our protocol, his and Jaxon's phone and guns were confiscated prior to their entrance to my inner office. It didn't matter what code or form of security Cole had on his phone or if he'd deleted his messages from Boudreau, my men could crack it.

I had three of the best hackers and technology wizards. And unlike Cole, they hadn't let me down—yet.

I looked over at Noah and offered a quick nod.

This conversation was done.

The verdict was in.

We'd learn whatever else we needed through Cole's phone and after a sweep of his apartment. This message would also go out on loudspeaker. I took a quick glance at Jaxon who was doing his best to appear competent enough as a leader to be present at this meeting.

It was a good thing Cole wasn't married. Leaving some woman a widow made me feel bad—only for a second or two. Truly, the women were usually better off. If someone came on my radar who I needed to be eliminated, that person was a piece of shit to begin with. Nevertheless, no woman was about to be a widow today.

I nodded to Noah who joined us standing.

*Guilty as charged.*

My hand landed on Cole's shoulder. "Come with me."

*Sentence to be carried out immediately.*

"Boss?" Jaxon asked.

"You're good where you are," I replied.

Beneath my touch, Cole Kensington trembled. It wasn't visible, but under my hand I felt his tremors. He wasn't the first and wouldn't be the last to react. Men—or women—in his current situation were capable of many things, and often their bodies betrayed their feigned show of strength. My goal was to get Cole out of my office, off my expensive rug, and into the kill room before he pissed himself...or vomited.

Damn, I hated vomit.

Noah pushed a button. The wall opened. It wasn't the doorway to the outer office. No, this sliding door opened to a small room, one that was currently too dark to adequately see.

They said that truth was stranger than fiction. However, my experience was that there was a lot of truth to be found in fiction. Take the television series *Dexter*, for instance. Plastic sheeting was extremely useful when containing blood splatter—or all bodily excretions.

I patted Cole's back as he took a step ahead of us. The plastic crackled under his boots and he stopped and looked down. Flipping a switch, I revealed a room a little larger than a closet and completely covered in plastic.

"What?"

In my experience when a person feared death or retribution for their ineptitude, they either refused to see what was right in front of them or simply couldn't compute. Eventually, they figured it out, but there was always a moment, subjective in length for each individual, when confusion obstructed their comprehension that their life was over.

Prolong that moment and it was the time begging and bartering began.

Between the continued vibration of my phone and the fact there was nothing I wanted from Cole Kensington, today there would be none of that. I took a small step back.

The pop from Noah's firearm preceded Cole's demise by milliseconds.

Red splattered over the plastic-covered walls. Cole Kensington crumpled much like one of those blow-up decorations people put in their yard, after someone pulled the plug. As we looked down, liquid turned his jeans dark as his bladder lost control.

"Get him out of here and find out if we can unload the Jag." I turned back to Jaxon. "I'm going to assume you'll be better at informing me, either directly or through Mr. Herbert or Mr. Trahan?"

Jaxon stood, nodding as his wide eyes took in Cole's body.

This wasn't the first dead man Jaxon had seen or even the first cold-blooded murder he'd witnessed. It was his first lesson in Ramses loyalty, one he wouldn't soon forget and would most likely broadcast far and wide.

That was my plan.

Two of my men were dead by my hands over Boudreau's doings. I didn't think my message could be clearer: work with him and die.

At least I had Emma safe and could concentrate on other shit.

"Jaxon, help me," Noah said as he tilted his head toward the body. There would be a process of wrapping the corpse in the plastic currently attached to the floor, walls, and ceiling. The body would be removed and disposed of. The room would be sanitized and new plastic would be hung. There was no good way to predict when it would be needed again.

My grandfather's notes had discussed preparedness at some length.

I reached for my phone.

Fuck, I'd not only missed a few calls and multiple messages, but our advanced security system had been activated.

Before calling or connecting to the camera history, I read the texts from Ian.

*"EMMA IS GONE."*

*"I WILL FIND HER, BOSS."*

*"THE KITCHEN DOOR SENSOR ACTIVATED."*

*"SHE WAS IN THE CARRIAGE HOUSE."*

I hit the call button as I opened the door to the

outer office. While Noah was aware of my houseguest, Jaxon Cormier wasn't. The office beyond was empty as my call to Ian connected.

"What the hell do you mean *was*? Talk to me." *Or you will fucking die.*

The last part was implied.

# EMMA

### Earlier

The man from the SUV in the garage walked out onto the sidewalk and looked both directions, most likely trying to learn what or who had activated the garage door to rise. Two more steps my direction and I'd be caught. With my body trembling, I watched him through a thick hedge of green with pink flowers. As I did, a bumblebee buzzed near one of the flowers and made a circle around my head.

My hand came to my lips as I stifled a scream.

When I looked back toward the garage, the man was gone, and by the sound reverberating through the air, the garage door was again descending.

Relief flooded my circulation as I let out my breath and dropped to my knees.

It took me a second to realize that my hiding place

really wasn't one. I was on a cobblestone pathway between two hedges in front of an iron gate. I looked through the rungs up at a large stately home—Rett's neighbor. It was beautiful and well maintained. With three stories, a large wraparound porch, gingerbread woodwork, and balconies on the second floor, it was classic New Orleans style. I said a prayer someone was home.

With the wrought-iron gate rattling in my grasp, my only thought was getting inside and using a telephone. A flip of a latch and the old gate opened inward, the hinges creaking with each inch. Closing the gate behind me, I straightened my shoulders and walked toward the house.

As I approached the front porch, I considered my options. I could say I was a lost tourist. A quick look down at my bare feet and I realized it made that story a bit unbelievable. I moved my head from side to side as my ears strained to hear and I looked and listened for someone—anyone—from Rett's house.

*Had they discovered I was missing?*

*What would happen when they did?*

My hope resided in the fact that Ian didn't knock too often. It was long before dinner, if Rett had intended to come and get me. I was without a watch, but I guessed it was midafternoon. Ian may not discover that I was MIA until after I was away.

Climbing the steps to the front porch, I made the decision that telling anyone that I'd been kidnapped and held in their neighbor's home wasn't a viable explanation either. I contemplated my options. Despite my fleeing, I had no desire to cause Rett legal problems. My yearning was to forget this bizarre chain of events and get back to my life.

Rapping my knuckles against the front screen door, I came up with a plausible story for my missing shoes. I'd been wearing high heels. They hurt my feet, so I removed them and accidentally left them in the park. I tried to remember the name of the park near the church.

No, that park was in the French Quarter, and as I looked around at the elegance and majesty of the homes, I knew I was no longer there. After another look behind me at the empty street and sidewalk, I knocked on the door again and continued my wait.

My nerves kicked up as I knocked a third time. When no one answered, I took a step closer to one of the tall windows.

With my pulse thumping in my ears, I shielded the sunshine with my hand to see through the glass pane. Condensation formed on the glass from my too-rapid breaths. Wiping it away, I squinted my eyes to see inside.

The room I saw was similar to Rett's dining room, with a heavy overelaborate table, upholstered tall-backed chairs, and a large chandelier light fixture. Everything within was immaculate and luxurious. The people who lived here would help me. I knew they would, if only they'd answer the door.

I turned, looking onto the street as a car drove slowly by. There were more houses, all very nice and maintained. However, I feared that if I continued house by house down the street, Rett, Ian, or another one of his men would surely see me.

It was then I thought of Kyle.

My mouth felt dry as I considered the possibility that all Rett had been telling me was true.

*What if the man who I'd known my entire life really wanted me dead?*

No. Kyle had died. I hadn't seen his body or those of our parents. The police said I could but warned me that the car had exploded upon impact and the remains were not the people I loved. I chose to allow the coroner to do his job, and then I had all three cremated.

Just because I hadn't actually seen Kyle or our mother or father didn't change the fact they were deceased. Ever since arriving in New Orleans, I'd been a player in a bad dream—no, a nightmare—and if I could simply call Ross, I could make it out. My thoughts may seem naive, but after a week, I was desperate to hold onto some reality.

Another scan of the street beyond the hedges and iron fence let me know there wasn't a posse out to get me yet or at least not a visible one. Breathing too heavily, I hurried down the steps from the porch, and walking on the grass, I went around the side of the large house opposite of Rett's home. Lush landscaping obstructed my view as I danced over prickly objects on the ground and continued my trek to the back of the house. Taking one last look toward the street, I stepped around a corner of the house, nearing what I assumed was the backyard.

There wasn't a warning.

No noise or visual alert.

I didn't see anyone. I barely had time to scream as I fought as something dark came over my head.

My lungs burned. I feared I was on the verge of hyperventilation as I clawed at what seemed like a bag, now secured around my neck. Instinctively, I released whatever was over my head as I thrust out my hands. I'd been pushed down, face-first, toward the hard earth. A gust of air came from my lungs as I landed with a thud, saving myself by a millisecond with my outstretched hands. The remaining air rushed from my lungs as a heavy object landed in the middle of my back.

I turned my face to the side. The world was obstructed by the black bag.

Muffled noises beyond my head covering were difficult to distinguish. I thought I heard the sounds of exasperation over my own screams and gasps for air.

I couldn't push up. Whatever or whoever was on top of me had me pinned. And then my wrists were roughly seized—one by one—and secured behind me with a sharp tether.

It all happened so fast.

No matter how much thrashing or yelling I tried, I was no match for my captor. The more I pulled against the restraints, the more they tightened. The ones on my wrists felt as though they'd cut my skin as my fingers clawed to no avail.

Spots formed in my vision. Through very small holes in the fabric I was able to make out the green of the grass where I was pinned.

*Was there more than one person?*

Before I realized what had been done, my ankles were also bound. The same sharp tether was used to keep my legs from kicking independent of one another.

"Rett," I called out, but my voice was muffled by the bag. "Rett."

*Why had I decided to flee?*

My shoulders screamed in pain as I was lifted by my bound arms and slung over someone's shoulder. I couldn't see and no one else besides me had spoken, yet I was certain, based on my position, that it was a hard shoulder cutting into my stomach.

I tried to kick.

With my wrists behind me and ankles secured, my protest was closer to the flopping of a fish than any real fight. It didn't take long before my muscles grew weary in this position.

I could run for thirty minutes on the treadmill, yet fighting for my life and safety had me worn out in what was either seconds or hours. Nothing made sense.

"Do it."

I held my breath at the voice. My mind raced, trying to recognize who spoke, wishing it was Rett, and wishing I was still up in the suite. My body bounced with each step of the person carrying me. The shoulder in my diaphragm made it difficult to inhale.

My concentration went to filling my lungs with much-needed oxygen.

And then I felt it—a sharp pinch in my ass.

Visions of the bumblebees around the flowers came back to me.

The panic that had been coursing through my system seconds before subsided. My muscles relaxed as they lost their tension. Within the black bag, the world went away.

## EMMA

Noises registered before vision returned. It was as if I were trudging through a fog, a fog in the bayou. Every muscle strained. My body ached as if it had been battered. Each attempt to move was met with resistance and a deep ache and tenderness that radiated throughout my body.

My eyelids blinked.

A blindfold.

My heart leaped.

Rett. I was back with Rett.

Shaking my head brought excruciating soreness to my neck and shoulders. Even my jaw ached. It took a second for it to register that my mouth was held open with a gag. My tongue pressed against the now-wet material.

Something sharp poked beneath my chin. Reflexively, I moved away, lifting my chin. Despite the soreness within, I moved as far as I could from the sharpness. It didn't seem to matter for the sensation followed.

"I could cut her throat."

My heart seized. It wasn't a voice I recognized.

"He wants her alive."

*He?*

My entire body trembled to the rate of convulsions as I tested my ability to move. It didn't take long to realize that I was sitting up with my wrists and ankles bound to a chair. Gripping the arms, I tried to make it rock. As I did, a cold breeze suddenly blew from somewhere above, making me keenly aware of the air on my skin.

*Was I naked?*

I tried to speak, to make noises through the gag.

"She's waking up."

"He wants her alive. He didn't say we can't fuck her until she passes out again."

More gurgled sounds came as I tried to speak. The gag restricted my lips and my tongue. Everything came out as gibberish.

I wanted to say, "Please, let me talk to *him*, whoever him was."

Yet no matter how I tried, I couldn't articulate more than nonsense with the saturated gag. The more I was aware of it, the harder it was to not choke.

"Look at that pussy."

Hearing the lust in the man's voice churned bile in

my stomach. I desperately tried to swallow as I shook my head from side to side. The blindfold wasn't tied gently as Rett had done it before and after our meals. Each movement of my head pulled at my scalp as if my hair was tangled in the knot.

"Boss said no."

*Thank God.*

Whoever the boss was, I was certain that it wasn't Rett.

I knew somewhere deep in my convictions that he wouldn't approve if I was naked. And if the boss these men mentioned was Kyle, if my brother—or the man raised as my brother—was truly alive, I wanted to speak to him, to ask him what this was all about.

I would assure him that I held no designs on New Orleans.

My body flinched as something cold and sharp touched my breast.

"Watch her nipples. The bitch wants one of us to fuck her."

*No, asshole. I'm scared, not turned on.*

The sensation returned, this time to my other breast. Although I did my best to not react, laughter from both men bounced throughout the room.

"I'm fucking tired of watching and not touching. Take off the gag and make her suck us."

"That might work. He didn't say nothing about fucking her mouth."

My head thrashed back and forth as one of them

came closer. In my hyper state, the combined smell of body odor mixed with a sweet tobacco scent added to the revolt in my stomach.

I coughed as the gag was pulled from my mouth, leaving the spit-drenched material to fall around my neck like a disgusting necklace. After moving my jaw from side to side, I found my voice. "If either of you puts your dick in my mouth, I'm biting it off."

My face moved quickly to the right as an open palm slapped me hard and more male laughter bounced off the walls. A grasp of my hair and my neck snapped upward.

"Bitch, if you bite me, I'll pull those pretty teeth one at a time."

"She'll be real good at sucking then."

"You'll be busy mourning your manhood." I brought my lips together, braced for another slap, as my hair was released.

A loud noise rattled through the room, sending a chill over me. I tried to make out what I was hearing. There were too many sounds. Commotion continued and was then accompanied by rapid-fire pops. That's what they sounded like. It reminded me of the snap noisemakers I'd played with as a child.

My lips came together and my face inclined as warm liquid sprayed over me. Before that could register, something like a small blanket covered me.

"Rett?" I called into the abyss created by the blindfold.

Since I'd awakened tied to a chair, until this moment I hadn't considered what Rett's response might be. After all, this happened because I did what he'd told me not to do. "Rett?" I called a bit more apprehensively from behind the material covering my eyes.

Relief washed through me as warm lips met mine. They were familiar, firm, and strong. Though mine were bruised, I pushed back toward him, longing for a connection.

Strong hands framed my cheeks as he pulled away.

"Tell me they didn't hurt you—rape you."

Tears of relief flowed from my covered eyes as my head shook. "I was so scared." I had been. I hadn't faced that reality, but now with Rett's hands on my cheeks, the fear flowed through me, inciting more tears. "How long? What time is it?"

A kiss came to my hair. I wasn't certain why he continually did that, but the familiarity of it caused my body to tremble with relief.

"Too long, Emma, too long. It's late." His tone hardened with each sentence. "Decoys threw us off. You walked into a waiting trap, one we should have seen. More than those two men will die for what happened today."

"You're angry."

"I'm livid, Emma. Right now, seeing you like this, I want to hurt someone." He paused. "Someone else. I'm using all my restraint right now."

I nodded. "Please take me home."

Something cut the ties on my wrists and ankles. "I'm leaving the blindfold on."

"I want to see you."

"You don't need to see what I just did." Rett lifted each of my wrists. "Don't argue with me. Now isn't a good time."

Taking a deep breath, I nodded again.

"I'm going to put my t-shirt over you and get you to a doctor."

Warm, soft fabric came over my head. If I hadn't known this was Rett, I would now. The damp mustiness of the room disappeared as I was covered with the rich, spicy scent of Rett's cologne. One arm at a time, he helped me lift my arms through the armholes. With each movement, I tried to stifle the groans, but every effort caused pain. It radiated through my body as if my nerves were ready to spark and my bloodstream was filled with liquid fuel.

"Now lift your arms, Emma. I'm taking you home."

I did as he said, unable to stop the moans as he lifted me.

The sound of a thud came with a small jolt—was that a kick?

Rett's tone grew colder. "These bastards didn't suffer enough. If I could, Emma, I'd bring them back to fucking torture them slowly."

This was a glimpse into this complicated man.

Rett's words and his actions reflected a dichotomy.

His speech was vengeful and his tone emotionless, yet as he held me, his touch was gentle.

Laying my head to my side, I realized that Rett had literally given me the shirt off of his back. My cheek settled on his warm, bare chest as he carried me away from wherever we were.

I listened to Rett's shoes as they clicked over the flooring. In my other ear, his steady heartbeat slowed to normal from the accelerated beat when he'd first lifted me. It felt as though we'd stepped through a doorway.

Warm air replaced the air conditioning. We were outside. Though I couldn't see, I assumed due to the limited information on a timeline Rett had given that it was now night and the sky was dark.

"Miss North."

I turned toward the voice. "Ian, I'm sorry."

"No, miss, I should have been watching."

I shook my head. "I was wrong."

It wasn't Ian who replied. "You were."

My breath caught at Rett's tone.

Doors opened as Rett placed me on a cool leather seat and followed me into the vehicle. It was funny that being with him, safe at his side, I no longer had a desire to remove the blindfold. This covering of my eyes had come to mean I trusted him and at this moment, I did. As I leaned against him and his arm came around me, I didn't care about vision. "Thank you for saving me."

He didn't reply.

The vehicle began to move.

I lifted my chin as if to look up at Rett. I imagined his dark brown eyes and strong chin. "I'm sorry."

His finger came under my chin, holding my face in place as a kiss came to my lips and another to the top of my head. "Not as sorry as you will be."

"Rett, you have to understand how I felt when—"

His finger came to my lips. "Don't, Emma. Now isn't the time to make excuses. I'm a man of action, and you don't want that at this minute. You're safe and I'm trying to concentrate on that. I assure you that it isn't in your best interest to have me thinking beyond that fact."

I wasn't certain I understood. "What do you mean? What are you going to do?"

His arm around me tightened as his volume lowered to a whisper. "First, you'll be checked out by the doctor." Another kiss to my hair. "We'll get you cleaned and bandaged. We need to learn everything you can recall. Those men are no longer a threat, but you may have heard something. We need to learn what that is before you forget."

None of that sounded like anything to make me sorry.

"And when you're up to it" —he laid his other hand on my thigh— "I'm spanking your ass."

My head came away from him. "I told you I'm not a child."

"I wouldn't spank a child."

"I don't understand."

He gently seized my chin again as warm breath skirted over my face. "You, Emma, are an intelligent woman who did a dangerous thing. Once I'm done, you will remember that."

I wanted to say I would remember, yet... As I tucked my lip between my teeth, I couldn't help wonder how I could be so sore, relieved, and at the same time, intrigued.

## EMMA

*W*e had arrived to Rett's home through the underground garage. I recognized the decline in the road, the different scents once the car door opened, and the way Rett's voice echoed in the concrete cavern.

Despite my offers to walk, I remained cradled against his chest as he carried me up the cement stairs. The sounds around us changed as we entered his home. Over the last week, I'd learned to rely more on my other senses as my sight was limited. The world was filled with sensory input if only we took the time to be receptive.

Rett's step had more bounce as we moved from cement, to tile, to hardwood. Now, after climbing another set of stairs, his footsteps were muted, indicating that we were walking down a rug-lined hallway. A latch clicked as I imagined a door opening.

After a few more paces, Rett laid me on a soft bed. Without speaking, he covered my legs and torso with a blanket.

Although I tried to utilize scents and sounds, I couldn't identify our location. We hadn't traveled up another stairway. That meant we weren't on the third floor. I felt the warmth of his body as the bed dipped, and Rett reached for the blindfold. "Hold still, Emma."

Lifting my hand, I stopped him. "Before you do that, I want you to know that I trust you."

He made a noise similar to a scoff.

"I do, Rett. More than I realized."

"I wish I could say the same. After this stunt, I can't."

His response pierced me in a way that corporal punishment couldn't. The honest truth was that Rett was right. I hadn't given him reason to trust me. I'd ignored his repeated warnings and risked my own life as well as his and maybe others. I deserved his lack of trust —Ian's also.

"I'm sorry..." My repeated apology floated through the air unmet with a verbal response.

Sulking in my own doing, I didn't realize how long it was taking Rett to untie the blindfold. Meticulously, he worked to loosen the knot and free my hair. Every now and then, I tensed as he worked. Once I felt the blindfold come free, I began to turn toward him.

"Not yet."

It was all he said before working to untie the gag.

Somehow, I'd forgotten about the wet material, still around my neck. As he worked on that, I took in my unfamiliar surroundings. Soon, it too was gone.

Rett gently turned me until we were facing each other. Exhaling, he leaned forward until our foreheads met. "You need to keep trusting me, Emma. Keeping you safe has been my only objective."

Sighing, I looked down. "I'm sorry that you had to save me."

He lifted my chin. "I'm not."

"You're not?"

Rett released me and sat taller. "I'm upset at what you did. I'm disappointed, but I'm not sorry for coming after you, for saving you from whatever those vile men had planned, and for stopping your ending up at the mercy of your brother." His head shook. "Just imagining those outcomes makes me see red." He lifted my arm, looking down at the red droplets. "Blood. Never doubt that I'll shed it without hesitation to keep you safe. I'll hunt down and punish anyone who puts you in danger."

My eyes opened wider. As they did, I could feel the tenderness and swelling on my right cheek. Squinting, I lifted my hand to gingerly touch the tender skin.

Rett took my hand and kissed my fingers. "You're guilty too, Emma. You put yourself in danger as much as those men who died tonight did." His nostrils flared as he took a deep breath. "We'll discuss your punishment later."

"I am sorry." When he didn't reply, I went on, "Those men are dead because of me."

"Those men are dead *tonight* because of you. They work for your brother and would have been killed one day."

I tried to grapple with the reality that I was living in a world where punishment was death and tonight I had been responsible for the deaths of two men. Rett pulled the trigger but only because of me and my doing. "How many times can I apologize?"

Rett shook his head and with a deep breath, stood. The stress of the day and night showed in his handsome face. His features were more prominent, his brow more pronounced, his eyes darker, and his chin more defined. He was a statue of a man, one I'd disappointed and longed to help.

"Emma, apologies are superfluous. You're saying you're sorry to make yourself feel better. It's time you faced the fact that we don't live in a world where apologies hold power. This is the real world. This is your life now.

"You said not to treat you like a child and yet you continue to act like one. Children lack the understanding of cause and effect. They think that they can say the magic words, I'm sorry, and the world continues to spin. It's a childish notion. Adults realize that apologies don't right wrongs. That takes action."

Rett resumed his seat on the side of the bed and lifted my chin with the soft grasp of his finger and thumb. "You can't bring those men back, and if you could, you wouldn't want that. Your apologies are wasted breath, a way to absolve yourself of your role in what happened. If you're looking for forgiveness, I can't and won't grant it."

Tears blurred my vision of Rett's stern expression. "What can I do?"

"Life is a ruthless teacher. Today I hope you learned something."

I nodded in his grasp. "I did."

I had learned more than one thing. I'd learned I was safest here with the man I didn't really know, but the more I learned about him, the more I wanted to know. I also learned that the dangers Everett Ramses warned me about were real. I'd been forced to recognize that the life I'd once had was gone. Rett was right: this was now my life. "I don't like all I've learned," I said honestly, "but I have learned."

"Then stop apologizing and concentrate on not repeating poor decision making."

My head and heart ached. My body was tender and sore. I may not be able to change the past, but in this moment, I wanted to think about anything else.

Sighing, I again took in the unfamiliar setting. We weren't in my suite. "Where are we?"

Compared to the suite where I'd been staying, this one was...grander. It was hard to pinpoint the differences. The floral pattern was gone, replaced by feminine decor in shades of creams and golds. Things looked newer and still splendid. Peering up and around, I scanned the tall golden walls, took in the craftsmanship of the white trim, and noticed the luxurious fabrics. The artwork on the walls hung in heavy frames. Under the area rug was a gleaming wood floor.

My gaze went toward the windows and my heart leapt. Though the sun had set, there were no closed shutters. I could see beyond the panes to lights coming from a story below.

"The windows aren't blocked," I said.

The large bed and bedside stand seemed to be the only real pieces of bedroom furniture. Much like the library where I'd been, one wall was a floor-to-ceiling bookcase filled with more books. On the opposite side of the room with its own area rug was a fireplace, currently unlit, and a sofa with small tables and chairs.

In one of the corners near the windows was a slightly larger table, round, with drop leaves and two chairs. A grin came to my lips as I noticed Rett's standard single red rose in a silver vase. Around the perimeter of the room were multiple doors—all closed.

While I'd been looking around, Rett had been closely examining my wrists and ankles.

"Ouch."

His dark stare moved from the injuries to my eyes. I tucked my lip between my teeth.

Rett's expression—clenched jaw, furrowed brow, and

tightening muscles—displayed his mood more accurately than his touch.

Without a word, he reached for my chin and turned my face from side to side. "I fucking meant it. I shouldn't have killed those bastards. Their demise was too easy."

I reached for Rett's hand, intertwining our fingers.

As I did, I noticed the dirt under my ragged nails and the dried blood around my wrist. Upon my arm were the red dots he'd referred to earlier. Ignoring the queasiness that the sights conjured in my stomach, I looked up at Rett as tears swelled upon my lids. "I know you said it doesn't help, and you're right. But I am sorry. I don't think I believed you. I didn't think that the danger you'd warned me about was real." Before he could speak, I went on. "I was more focused on getting away. My plan was to call Ross. And then I could go back to being me."

"You are you, Emma. I haven't asked you to be anyone else."

"You have, and I don't..." My head moved from side to side. Now wasn't the time to discuss what I thought he wanted from me. "If you're okay with me being me, don't lock me away."

Rett stood. This time, he paced away from the bed toward the windows and back. With his shirt still missing, I watched the muscles in his toned torso tighten and his neck straighten. His bicep bulged as he ran his hand over his face. When he spun back toward me, I saw the exhaustion in his dark stare. He lifted his hand toward me. "Look what happened to you." His volume rose. "Don't you get it? I'm not locking you away. I am trying to keep you safe."

The tears that had teetered on my lids now cascaded down my cheeks. No matter how fast I swallowed, I couldn't rein them in. "I get it." I laid my head back, groaning as my temples throbbed. "I get it." The tears burned my eyes as I stared up, not focusing on the ornate woodwork. Turning to Rett, I asked, "Why?"

## EMMA

"Why?" My one-word question hung in the air.

It was at that moment when everything came together—everything: the anxiety of my escape, the shock of my kidnapping, and the terror of waking as I had with those men. Pulling my knees to my chest, I ignored the pain, wrapped my arms around my legs, and gave into the surge of emotion. My body convulsed as sobs brewed within me.

Hell, this breakdown was about more than what had happened today.

It was a week of being strong, of taking my life an hour at a time, and a day at a time. It was all too much and now pain had been added to the mixture. My chest heaved as I shed tears into the blankets.

I didn't know how long my outburst lasted, but when I looked up, Rett was no longer across the room.

He'd taken a seat on the edge of the big bed. With my nose and more tears running, I looked up. "Why does Kyle want me dead?"

With his thumb, Rett wiped one cheek and then the other before handing me a tissue.

"Thank you."

He watched me for a moment before speaking. No longer was there anger in his tone. "In order for Kyle's claim to New Orleans royalty to have a chance to work, he must convince others that he is the rightful heir of Isaiah Boudreau. Some might ask how anyone could make such a claim, but New Orleans is a world where legends and lore create history. Some are accurate. Other tales are just that, stories that have been told so many times that they become real.

"Kyle's claim is based on a truth. Nearly twenty-seven years ago, Jezebel North conceived Isaiah Boudreau's bastard child. The greater parishes of New Orleans saw her, listened to the rumors, and knew her child was Boudreau's.

"Kyle claims to be that child." Rett's head shook. "He isn't. The dates of his birth and yours are eight months apart. He is too old. In reality, you are too young. Nevertheless, we know that you are that child, Emma. You are the illegitimate child of Jezebel and Isaiah. You see, Isaiah's wife never conceived. That made you even more special. If you exist, you threaten the authenticity of his story."

A cold chill ran over me. "How do you know it's me?"

"It doesn't matter. We just know."

"Maybe I'm not the right person and this can all end."

Rett's shoulders squared.

I reached over and laid my hand on his arm. "Maybe not you and me, but if I'm no longer a threat, I'm no longer in danger. We could start over like normal people."

Rett turned quickly my direction. "Normal is average, commonplace." His tone grew gruffer as if his patience with me was waning. "*You* are not average nor am I. We were born to be royalty. Not the figureheads who ride in carriages and wave at the crowds. Emma, you were conceived to be a queen. Your mother understood the danger you were in and gave you up to the O'Briens."

"How are you so sure? Children are adopted every day. Maybe I was born to someone else. The attorney gave me some information, but none of it was substantiated."

Rett's phone vibrated and he looked down and then up. "The doctor is here."

"Rett, tell me."

Inhaling, he sat taller. "It was you, Emma. You are the child of Jezebel and Isaiah, and you were the one who made it known to the world. You are here today because you publicized your connection a few months after Kyle made his claim."

"I did no such thing." I was adamant. "How could I make something known that even I didn't know?"

"You did one of those ancestry kits."

My eyes widened as my heart beat faster. "Oh God, I did."

"Your lineage wouldn't have been public if you hadn't done that."

"No." I lay back against the pillows. "I'd forgotten about that kit. It was a gift. I remember thinking that since I hadn't known I was adopted until after the O'Briens were gone and unable to answer my questions, I figured maybe I'd learn something."

"A gift?"

"Yes."

"Who gave you the gift?" Rett asked.

I thought back. "It was odd. It arrived after Christmas. I thought the kit was from Ross's girlfriend at the time—ex-girlfriend. I think her name was Jenn. The three of us had joked about the kits once and I assumed it was her." I thought back. "No, her name wasn't Jenn. It was Emily. I remember teasing Ross that her name was close to mine."

"Why would you think she sent it?"

"She and Ross broke up right before Christmas, so I couldn't ask her to be sure. And when I asked, Ross said it wasn't from him, which, by the process of elimination, left her. As I said, it arrived a few weeks after Christmas. At first, I ignored it. It just sat there. Then one day, I thought, what the heck?" My mind tried to recall. "Rett, the results never came. You're supposed to get a package or something, an email, something. I never did. Honestly, I'd forgotten all about that kit."

He stood. "Tell me more about Emily."

I shrugged. "Ross and I had an agreement to not bring up his exes. He moved from one to the other without consideration for abandonment of the last one."

"Emily. Describe her."

Rett seemed oddly focused on her. "I don't know...red hair. Pretty. Nothing special. Not much to tell."

"Her last name?"

A smile tugged at my lips. "Ross wasn't great at remembering last names and that caused a bit of trouble more than once. But hers, I remember..."

"Could it have been Oberyn?"

That was it.

I sat up as a knock came to the door. "How would you know that?" I asked.

"That's probably the doctor," Rett said, not answering my question. "She is in a practice with another doctor here in New Orleans who I trust immensely."

"So you trust her?"

"I do and after this evening, I'd kill any other man who looked at you."

My smile returned. "Then I'm glad she's a woman." As Rett began to walk toward the door, I asked again. "Where are we?"

"This is your real suite, Emma. The other one was temporary." He pointed to one of the doors. "It connects to mine." He turned away but continued to speak. "The closets, drawers, and racks are filled. Ian said you weren't ready. Deal with it. Don't argue. This is where you'll remain."

I swallowed my response.

Rett turned the knob and opened the door. "Dr. Dustin."

"Mr. Ramses." A petite young woman with dark hair pulled back in a ponytail entered. She smiled my direction politely without acknowledging my state of injury and disarray. "I hear that I have a patient in here."

"Yes," Rett said, gesturing toward me, "this is Emma. Emma, this is Dr. Gloria Dustin."

In the doctor's hand, she had a bag, much like the kind doctors carried for house calls. That made sense. We were in a house.

"Emma, I'm happy to see you're awake."

"Sore," I said, "but awake."

"Have you eaten?"

"We thought it best," Rett answered, "to wait for you to clear her."

Dr. Dustin turned to Rett. "Mr. Ramses, thank you for calling for me. Now, if you'll excuse us."

My eyes widened. "He can stay."

Dr. Dustin spoke to him. "If you stay nearby or leave me your number, I'll let you know when you can return. I need some time alone with my patient. I'm sure you understand."

A grin came to my lips. Despite Dr. Dustin's small frame, she had the gumption to ask Rett to leave a room in his own home. I liked her already. When Rett's gaze came to mine, I nodded. "I'll be fine. I promise."

He looked down at his bare chest. "I could use a shower. Once I'm done, I'll be back."

Rett walked my direction. Pausing, he lifted my hand. His eyes went to the doctor and back. "You're in good hands, Emma. Dr. Dustin wouldn't be here if she wasn't loyal to the Ramses name."

I nodded as he planted a kiss on my hair.

Dr. Dustin and I waited until Rett disappeared, not through the door she'd entered, but the one he'd earlier indicated went to his suite. After the door closed, she came closer. "Emma, I was given some information about your injuries. Can you tell me more?"

My lip went between my teeth, weighing what I should and shouldn't say.

"I need to treat you," she said. "To treat you, I need as much information as you can give me. Whatever you say is confidential, covered under doctor-patient privilege."

"I was taken."

"By Mr. Ramses?"

I curled my lips into a grin because in reality she was correct. "No. I don't know who." I lifted my wrists. "They must have drugged me. When I woke, I was tied to a chair."

She inspected my wrists. "It looks like they used zip ties. The plastic can be very sharp."

*Was it odd that she knew that?*

"I don't know what they used. I was also blindfolded and gagged."

"Mr. Ramses was the one who saved you?"

I nodded. "He was."

"I can assume these perpetrators are in police custody?"

While I was very new at this life, a bit of my naiveté from earlier in the day had been lost in today's lessons. "You could assume anything, Dr. Dustin."

"Thank you for being honest with me, Emma. Now, tell me, can you walk? I'd like to help you to the bathroom. The light in there will be better, and I need to see everything." She lifted my hand. "If it would be helpful to the police, we can take samples under your fingernails and see if there is any DNA they have on record."

"Would you pass it on to the police?"

"That is the usual chain of evidence." She tilted her head. "My partner, Dr. Thomas Bidwell, mentioned that

Mr. Ramses prefers to deliver evidence to the authorities himself."

"We should do that," I said.

"Okay. After I check you over and we get any samples, we can work together to clean you up and care for your injuries. I have some medicine and bandages, assuming you don't need anything more complicated."

Grimacing, I pulled back the covers. "Oh."

My legs were covered with red speckles. I hadn't seen them before. I lifted my arms, seeing the fainter red dots that we'd talked about earlier. A recollection of pops and the spray of warm liquid—blood—returned. My stomach lurched.

"Emma, are you all right? You became very pale."

I nodded. "I think getting cleaned up is a good idea."

With Dr. Dustin's help and still wearing Rett's shirt, I got out of bed. Then I stopped, looking at the remaining doors. "You're going to think I'm crazy" — and I probably was— "but I don't know which door is the bathroom."

"May I?"

I nodded.

Leaving me in place, Dr. Dustin went to the first door, the one nearest the entry, opened it, and turned on the light. "I found it."

# EMMA

When the doctor and I entered the bathroom, which not surprisingly was even nicer than the one upstairs, the first thing I noticed was my reflection. I stood for a moment—Rett's t-shirt falling to above my knees—wondering if the woman in the mirror was really me. She moved when I moved, tilted her head when I did, and her bloodshot eyes followed mine. Yet we were detached from one another.

I tugged at a small twig lodged in my disheveled blonde hair as I continued to scan my likeness. Trails of tears had left lines going down my dirty cheeks and red speckles covered my skin. I searched for the woman I'd seen in the morning.

*Was she under all this grime?*

It was more than my reflection. I felt different inside.

*Would that change?*

I couldn't describe the sensation as I looked closer at the purple swelling on my cheek. No wonder it had held Rett's attention. Tenderly, I prodded the inflamed skin. Each point of pressure sent a dull diffusion of pain through my nervous system.

"Is this the first time you've seen yourself since being home?" Dr. Dustin asked.

My mind churned with her question.

*Most remarkably, I wondered, am I home?*

"Emma." The doctor stepped closer. "We can do this away from the mirror if it would be easier."

Swallowing new tears, I shook my head. "I'm okay."

"You are, but it's acceptable for you not to be." She pulled out the small stool at the dressing table. "Come sit for a minute."

My energy to disagree was spent. Mindlessly, I went to the chair and sat.

"I have names of people you can talk to."

I shook my head again. "I'm just really tired."

"I'm sure you are. Let's get started. First, can you show me your hands?"

I lifted them in the air, turning them one way and the other. The first things I noticed were my wrists. It was as if someone had cut all the way around each one, as if leaving me with dried-blood bracelets. Next, I concentrated on my nails. The first night Rett came to get me for dinner I'd painted them a soft pink. Not only was the polish chipped, but many of my nails were broken, leaving a rough edge. My palms were also dirty, and near my thumbs the skin was sore.

Dr. Dustin spoke as she did her work. I liked listening although I couldn't be sure of what she'd said. Whatever it was took my thoughts away, listening to her story, as she completed her tasks. First, she cleaned under each nail, meticulously placing the dirt and debris in a small bag. She even clipped the rough edges, saving the clippings. Next, she scraped some of the dried blood from my skin, not mine from my wrists and ankles but the droplets that had splattered over me. After removing Rett's shirt, the doctor thoroughly inspected my skin, asking questions as she worked. She found small cuts near my nipples and a few under my chin.

It was her next request that made my hands tremble. I should have expected it, and yet there was no way to mentally prepare. Laying a plush towel on the floor, she asked me to lie down on my back. As I made my way to the floor, I knew this was why Rett requested a female doctor.

It wasn't as if I had never had a gynecological exam before. It was the memory of the way I'd been tied to the chair that caused the new onslaught of tears as she completed her exam.

"Emma, I don't see any signs of trauma. I would need to take samples for sperm or spermicidal substances. Do you believe you were raped?"

"No," I answered honestly. "I remember them talking about wanting to."

"I can do a rape kit if you want. It's your decision."

Struggling to hold back more tears, I replied, "I want this to be over."

"I will only run a few tests to be sure there's been no disease transmission." When she was done, Dr. Dustin smiled and nodded. "Let's turn on the shower. You'll feel better."

She was right. The water coming down was like no shower I'd ever taken. I could have stood under the multiple showerheads for days, allowing the warm liquid to wash over me. I washed my hair and added conditioner. Using a loofah and bodywash, I cleaned myself. Without Dr. Dustin's prompting, I may have scrubbed away a layer or two of skin. When I brushed my teeth, the corners of my lips burned from the toothpaste. We decided it had been the gag that had caused them to split.

Over an hour after Dr. Dustin arrived, I was examined, cleaned, and my wrists, ankles, and multiple cuts were covered in medical creams and bandaged. Dr. Dustin started me on an antibiotic regimen to ward off infection. She prescribed some mild painkillers. Without x-rays, she believed that I had bruised but not broken ribs. There were multiple other areas of bruising including my cheek, which she assured me would heal. She said that if any of the pain worsened, I was to contact her, and she'd follow up with more tests.

I didn't mention that my ability to contact her was contingent upon Rett. There were too many things going through my mind to contend with something as trivial as my phone. Funny, a day ago, not having a phone hadn't seemed trivial.

When we opened the door to the bedroom suite, Rett was waiting. His chest was now covered with a soft navy-blue t-shirt. His dirty blue jeans from earlier were replaced with a new pair of blue jeans. And his wavy hair was combed back and still wet from his shower.

As the doctor and I entered, Rett stood, his stubbly jaw set and his intense dark stare searching, scanning me as if there were a message written on me that only he could see.

I pulled the soft white chenille robe tighter.

"Emma."

"I'm good."

I wasn't. I knew that, but my desire for discussion was replaced by the combination of fatigue and sadness.

With my wet long hair combed and hanging down my back and wearing only the robe, I walked to the sofa near the fireplace and sat, unsure what would happen next. As Rett and Dr. Dustin began to converse, I took a small bit of comfort in the fact that I'd given the doctor permission to share any medical findings or information with Rett. Honestly, I wasn't sure if my permission was necessary in my new existence where Everett Ramses ruled; nevertheless, authorizing their discussion gave me a smidgen of control in a world where I felt it slipping away.

My mind wandered as the two of them discussed her findings and recommendations for my recovery. I heard bits and pieces, such as that the doctor Rett knew better was Thomas Bidwell. Dr. Dustin was his associate or vice versa. It didn't matter. Just before she was about to leave, Dr. Dustin handed Rett a manila envelope. "This is evidence."

As he looked at the envelope, his posture changed, growing more rigid by the second. It was then that I realized I hadn't heard them discuss the gynecologic findings.

"Rett," I called from across the room.

Instead of looking my way, he lifted his hand to still me and continued his unrelenting stare at Dr. Dustin.

"Evidence of..." He left the sentence open-ended.

"I would assume the perpetrators," she responded. "Thomas mentioned that you prefer to provide NOPD with the evidence yourself. While that is unusual, I agreed to that as well as the other terms upon taking Emma as a patient.

"There are scrapings from beneath Emma's fingernails." She smiled my way. "I think she gave them hell." Her expression turned serious as she turned back to Rett. "And there are also samples of the blood that was on her skin. There is enough for a DNA match if that's needed for trial."

"Anything else?" he asked.

"You and Emma can discuss that."

Rett remained rigid, still not looking my way. "Yes, Doctor, thank you." He lifted the envelope. "We never know what will be needed at trial. You're right. Emma deserves justice. The men who did this deserve to pay."

"Emma," Dr. Dustin said, again looking my direction, "call me if anything changes. For now, my advice is to eat what you can, drink plenty of fluids, and rest as much as possible."

I nodded.

"Thank you, Doctor," Rett said, opening the door. "This is Miss Guidry; she'll walk you to your car." Dr. Dustin nodded as she disappeared. He paused and then said, "Just a minute," before closing the door. His eyes narrowed as he turned my way. "What isn't she saying, Emma?"

I shook my head very slightly. "I didn't hear all she said."

He came closer, his presence looming over me. "What should we discuss?"

I could have stood to put myself on more equal footing, literally and figuratively, but I didn't. "I tried to tell you when she was here. You didn't want to hear it."

"I want to hear it now."

"There's nothing to discuss."

His lips formed a straight line as he continued his laser-focused stare.

# EMMA

"*I*'m waiting." His deep voice rumbled through the suite.

"Dr. Dustin checked me, as you undoubtedly knew she would..."

Rett's footing shifted as an awkward silence settled around us. "What did she learn?"

"What I already told you—they didn't rape me."

His chest deflated as he let out a long breath, and without another word, he returned to the door and opened it. A moment later, Ian entered wheeling a cart with two large silver domes as well as beverages.

"Come eat, Emma," Rett said as if my answer had given him permission to drop the other conversation completely.

Ian began to move the dishes to the small table.

As I started to stand, the room lost balance and I sat back against the soft sofa. I reasoned my dizziness was due to the recent medication taken on my empty stomach. It wasn't only the drugs that caused me to sit. Despite a painkiller the doctor had given me, my muscles seemed to stiffen by the minute.

Rett continued speaking to me as he helped Ian situate our dinner. "And after we're done eating, you're coming with me to my office. Ian will be there and two others of my trusted men. I want you to tell them everything that you remember."

The combination of the day's trauma, pain medicine, and shower worked as a sedative. With my elbow on the arm of the sofa, I rested my head on my hand. "I'm tired. Can't that wait until tomorrow?"

Heck, it could already be tomorrow. I hadn't seen a clock.

"No," Rett said without further explanation.

I sat still as Ian took the cart away.

Rett gestured again for me to come over to the table.

*Was this another time I wasn't supposed to argue?*

I decided it was, not because of Rett as much as my exhaustion.

With a deep breath I stood, wincing as I steadied myself, my fingers gripping the back frame of the sofa. Closing my eyes, I let myself adjust to the soreness as the room steadied. When I opened my eyes, Rett was beside me, his arm around my waist. The scent of his shower gel surrounded us in a cloud of freshness.

"Let me help you."

I did, walking with him to the table. Just before sitting, I looked out the tall window. My smile formed as I took in the fountain below. "I see it."

"What do you see?" he asked as he helped me with the chair.

"The Ramses family crest. I couldn't see it when we were in the courtyard, but from here, with the lights from the fountain, I can."

While the food before me smelled wonderful, the medication had my stomach in knots. Unexpectedly, my hand shook as I lifted the glass of ice water. I steadied it with my other hand as I brought it to my lips. The bandages peered out from under the cuffs of the robe. After setting the glass down, I noticed Rett's dark stare. He hadn't even lifted a utensil.

"You need to eat," he repeated. "Dr. Dustin said that."

"My stomach is upset. I think it might be the antibiotics and painkiller."

Rett pulled out his phone. "Tell me what sounds good. I'll call the kitchen and have it brought up."

I looked down at the white fish covered in parmesan cheese and fresh green beans. "That's silly. This is good food. Besides, it's late."

"It's early if you want to be technical."

No wonder I was tired. I wasn't asking someone to create a new meal at whatever time it was in the morning.

I lifted my fork. "Then the cook can go to bed. I'll

eat this." I cut a small piece of the fish. It was flaky and perfectly done. After a few bites, I looked across the table. Rett too had begun to eat. "I know you're upset with me."

He nodded. "I told you I was."

"But you're being...nice."

Rett laid down his fork and leaned back against the chair. "Don't misinterpret what I'm being. I'm not nice. We can settle that discussion right now. What I'm being is measured. I won't bore you with my last twenty-four hours, but let me say, the two men in that warehouse weren't the only in that time period to die by my hand."

Now I set my fork down. My stomach twisted with his honesty. "Why?"

"A better question might be why I didn't follow through on my original promise. Do you recall the one I made to you at the restaurant?"

I inhaled and did my best to appear strong. "You said you'd not let Kyle kill me."

Rett's lips curled in a menacing grin as he lifted the napkin to dab the corners of his mouth. "My dear, you have a way with words. I can see why you aspire to be an author." He stood and walked behind me. Each step upon the wood floor was accentuated by the tap of his shoes. The sound gave me the sensation of drumbeats, signaling a coming change.

Though my neck straightened, I didn't turn but

instead remained forward, much like the night at the restaurant.

"I believe," Rett said, "I told you that I'd kill you myself before I allowed Kyle to take your life." His hands came to my shoulders, caressing with his powerful fingers. "Your behavior today almost robbed me of the ability to fulfill that promise." His fingers moved up, walking like a tiny army, under my long hair and around my neck, yet there was no pressure. Moving my hair to the side, he leaned forward, his next question bringing warm breath to my sensitive skin. "Come, Emma, do you think I'm happy about that?"

"No," I said resolutely. "I know you're not."

"Do you think that when I saw you, the woman who was born to be my wife, naked and tied to a chair, that the only people I thought to kill were the two ignorant assholes who made a deadly mistake by touching you?"

Beneath the robe, my skin chilled.

Rett's fingers moved higher up my throat, lifting my chin. "You are a queen, and the way they had you positioned..." He brought my chin higher. "For longer than I care to admit, I considered firing three bullets."

"But—"

He pushed my mandible higher, stopping my rebuttal. "I did, Emma. I'm not a good man. You may be an angel, but I'm the devil. Never forget that. You almost lost your life today, yes from Kyle, but more interestingly, at my hands." His grip was still present like a heavy collar.

His positioning wasn't the threat of impending violence; it was the reminder that violence was a possibility.

Releasing my neck, Rett spun my chair toward him. No longer standing, he crouched in front of me. Without the gentleness he'd shown earlier, he flipped back my robe and spread my knees. "This pussy was on fucking display."

Keeping my neck straight, I gave him no resistance.

He spread my legs wider. "Do you have any idea what that did to me?"

"Rett—"

"No." His grip of my knees tightened as his volume rose. The one word reverberated through the new suite. His chest heaved with rapid breaths.

Keeping my head high, a tear slid down my cheek, but I didn't respond.

Rett leaned back on his haunches and released my knees.

I scrambled to bring my legs together and cover myself with the robe.

"Fuck," he mumbled as he ran his hand over his face.

In that instant, his expression changed. If I was to describe it, I'd say remorse supplanted rage.

As he stood, I reached for one of his hands and held it between both of mine. "You didn't hurt me."

"I fucking wanted to, Emma."

Swallowing and pushing past the sore muscles, I stood and met him chest to chest. "You've been nice because the alternative was..." I tried to find the right word.

"The alternative was taking your life." Rett brought his palm to my bruised cheek as his head shook. "I don't fucking know what to do with you."

Inclining my face toward his touch, I nodded. "I won't apologize again for what I did, but I will tell you that I learned many things today. One" —I laid my hand over his soft blue t-shirt— "is fear. Today, waking in that chair, in that position, and realizing I was naked" —my stomach twisted— "and hearing those men talk about me as if I weren't a person, as if I were an object, and the uncertainty of what would happen next..."

He lowered his hand and exhaled. "Emma, you don't—"

"*That* was fear, Rett." Speaking my feelings was liberating. "It was fear like I've never known. I thought I knew what it was like to be scared. I didn't. Today didn't compare. I remember being fearful of the unknown when my family died and I was left on my own, but I had people and friends in Pittsburgh. Today, or yesterday, I was alone as I've never before experienced. And I was vulnerable." The small hairs on the back of my neck stood up. "I didn't like it. I was terrified. I was frightened they'd kill me, and I was more afraid they wouldn't.

"You asked what seeing me in that position did to you. Let me tell you what it did to me." I took a step back. "It humiliated me. It reduced me to someone...less." Each phrase was uttered without hesitation. The conviction in my voice grew stronger. Only the new tears showed my weakness. "It dehumanized me. If you had taken that opportunity to fulfill your promise, to be the one to take my life...." I shook my head and crossed my arms over my breasts. "I would have died with those as my last thoughts. Or maybe it would have been a blessing, and I wouldn't have to live with the memories."

I lifted my chin and wiped the tears from my cheeks. "So I won't be thanking you again for saving me. The more I consider it, the less I'm convinced I have reason to be grateful."

Focusing on each tender step, I walked around him and reached for the chair to resume eating whatever my stomach could handle. Before I sat, Rett seized my arm and spun me toward him. Before I could process, I was backed against the window, the Ramses crest a story below filling my peripheral vision with colors. Rett's hands were on my ass, pulling my hips toward him. His face was inches from mine.

"I'm fucking grateful," he said. "I don't want you dead, Emma."

It was such a rudimentary sentiment—not wishing another's death, and yet it was my breaking point. I lifted my arms to his shoulders as my face fell to his wide chest. New tears dampened his t-shirt as my chest shuddered with sobs. His hold lightened, yet he didn't let me go, keeping me against him.

Finally, Rett spoke. I felt his words vibrating from his chest. "You are a queen—mine, New Orleans's. What happened today doesn't change that." He ran his hand gently over my back. "I will spend the rest of my life telling you that, Emma."

Sniffling, I tried to back away, but there was nowhere for me to go.

Rett held me tight. "I learned something today, too."

I looked up. "You did? Something besides not wanting to kill me."

He nodded. "A few things."

I waited.

"What you called nice wasn't easy."

"But you did it."

"I guess that's what I learned. I learned that while violence is my go-to response, I am capable of making exceptions." He leaned back until his gaze met mine. "I learned that *you* are that exception. What happened to you today...I saw it as an attack on me."

I started to speak but stopped as Rett went on.

"I did. I told you that I'm selfish. I am. I see life through one lens. That lens only views the world from my perspective. Today when we were coming up with dead ends and you were still missing, I was rabid. I wanted to hurt, needed to lash out."

The muscles of his arms tightened around me.

"Nothing has ever stopped me from acting on those impulses," he went on, "ever—until today. When we found you and it was confirmed you were inside, I didn't want anyone to see you. I didn't know what I'd find once I went through the next doorway or even if you were still alive. I just knew you were my responsibility, and your fate was in my hands." He took a deep breath. "I instructed my men to stay out, and I went in that room alone. That's crazy. Hell, it's the recipe for my death. I knew that. I knew it could have been a trap set by Kyle."

He exhaled. "You see, part of who I am, what I do, means I must stay protected. My men would die for me and I'd ask nothing less. When I'm out, no matter where I am, there are always men around me. Today I told them to stand back because of you. It fucking broke my heart to see you like that." He tilted his head. "Until today, I wasn't sure that organ existed within me."

My cheeks rose as I listened.

"Don't get any ideas. It broke because it's made of stone."

I again placed my hand over Rett's chest. "It's beating."

"And so is yours. Not only because I found you. It's beating because when those horrible thoughts were going through your mind, when you were afraid and degraded, you didn't give up." He smiled. "I heard you tell them what you'd do if either of them put his cock..."

"Yeah, I said I'd bite it off."

"That was the second I knew that with you, I had to react differently."

"Because you're afraid of me?" I asked with a grin.

"No, Emma, because I admired you...I do admire you. That doesn't mean you're off the hook. What you did today was stupid. It needs to be punished. For now, that punishment can wait."

"I think I've been punished."

"Not enough." Rett looked toward the table and pulled back my chair. "Try to eat. Talking to my men can wait until tomorrow."

"Thank you." I wasn't one hundred percent sure what I'd thanked him for.

Was it for his assistance in sitting?

Was it for his heartfelt honest reckoning?

Or was I grateful that I'd been saved?

Even with the horrible memories, I thought I was —grateful.

# EMMA

*D*ays and nights passed as I adjusted to my new suite and healed physically while simultaneously pushing away thoughts of what had happened. The suite had all the amenities of the one on the third floor with the added bonus of windows that opened and a door that led to Rett. The only deficiency was that being on the second floor, there wasn't a button that magically opened the ceiling. That was all right. I could open windows.

When Rett had said that this suite was filled with things for me, he didn't exaggerate. No longer did I need Ian to bring me dresses. I had a closet larger than the bedroom in my old apartment as well as dressers filled with clothes. There were clothes for every occasion. I also had a drawer devoted to jewelry. It was velvet lined and contained multiple small compartments. Each day I had another piece or two as

Ian or Rett would deliver what I now knew was not costume jewelry. There were also shoes of every color for every use. On the second day in this suite, I realized the exercise room was accessible from my suite as well as Rett's. I'd awakened to the sounds of his workout.

I'd lain under the blankets imagining that it wasn't a treadmill or range-of-motion machine that was pushing him to exhaustion. My thoughts were less fitness and more erotic. We'd fallen into a strange sort of relationship. I felt the spark or twinge of delight when we touched, and his kisses could reroute my circulation and leave me wanting more. And all the while, even with our suites connected, *more* hadn't come.

That first day I'd awakened in his home was the last time we'd been intimate, the last time I'd orgasmed without my own help. It wasn't that we were platonic; it was that we had stilled in that forward motion.

There was another win. The doors separating our suites as well as the one to the hallway weren't locked. I knew that by the sound they made whenever Rett or Ian entered or left. Nevertheless, I didn't try to open them or go beyond unaccompanied. It wasn't for lack of curiosity; it was something altogether different.

As for the hallway, I'd installed my own barrier. I'd breached it once, and I didn't want to do that again. When it came to Rett's suite, I didn't want to be there unless he wanted me there. Entering on my own felt a little like trespassing into his private space.

There were many reasons he might not want me

there. He was still busy dealing with fallout from my attempted escape. The morning after our heart-to-heart talk, I was escorted to his office. Escort was a nice way to say I was led with my eyes covered.

It would be a lie to say the blindfold didn't cause me to recall my abduction. It was also worth mentioning that Rett was the only one to place or remove it.

He had mentioned my affinity for words.

Rett was the master.

There was a quality to his tone when he expected to get his way. It wasn't brash or even demanding. It certainly wasn't asking. It simply was his style. In a way I appreciated that even after my ordeal, he believed I could handle the loss of sight.

I could, as long as he was there.

In Rett's office—a hidden room—I recounted all I could remember.

Because I'd arrived blindfolded, I was a bit startled when while seated at a long table, the wall opened. It was like something from the movies. A man named Leon entered. Once he was also seated, they asked me to tell them what had happened. I started with the accidental discovery that Ian was gone. As I spoke, Rett's men didn't look at me as if I had been the cause of Rett's wrath even though we all knew I had been. They were polite while questioning me about specifics as they tried to learn more. I told them that I'd heard a *he, him, or boss* mentioned but not a name.

Though Rett rarely mentioned Kyle, I knew it was

still Rett's mission to bring him down. After what had happened to me, his quest was even more determined.

Rett and I had resumed our dinners around his home.

If we ate in my suite, Ian brought the food. When we ate out and about—the dining room, courtyard, or conservatory—Miss Guidry made an appearance. Each encounter was an adventure. Rett finally explained her references to my biological mother. Miss Guidry was a spiritualist. She spoke to spirits or believed she did. I couldn't honestly tell which was true.

It was always a surprise who she would bring up. It wasn't only my birth mother; she often spoke of Rett's mother as well. Interestingly, she never mentioned Rett's father, although she frequently discussed Marilyn Ramses. Mrs. Ramses, or Miss Marilyn, as Miss Guidry referred to her, had been Miss Guidry's closest friend. It had been what I'd assumed in the story that I'd stopped writing.

Tonight, as we dined, Rett received a call, one he begrudgingly took, excusing himself and stepping away from the room. Upon his departure, Miss Guidry took the opportunity to speak privately with me.

She was giddy with excitement, her cheeks pink and a bounce in her step. "Miss North."

"Emma, please." It was hardly the first time I'd asked to be called by my first name.

The older woman sat on the edge of the seat Rett had vacated a few moments earlier. "Miss Emma, I couldn't wait to share something with you." Her expression dimmed. "Mr. Ramses doesn't appreciate when I talk too much about Miss Marilyn." Her smile returned. "But Lordy, she's been after me, waking me up..." Miss Guidry's head shook as she waved her hand. "She wants you to know that she approves."

My gaze went between the woman who had taken Rett's seat and the doorway, expecting his return. "She approves?"

"Of you and Mr. Ramses. She had reservations."

My mind went through a strange series of revelations.

Rett's deceased mother had reservations about me.

It was her son who found me.

When I didn't respond, Miss Guidry went on. "Now, it wasn't you she had reservations about. It's your daddy. Miss Marilyn never liked Mr. Boudreau. No, not one bit." Miss Guidry leaned forward and lowered her volume. "You see, she didn't much trust him. It wasn't that she had personal experience, but the ladies of society talk."

"How does she feel about my mother?" I almost giggled at my own question. I was asking this old woman about parents I never knew and only recently learned existed while speaking of the deceased in the present tense.

Miss Guidry's lips came together. "There are some subjects refined ladies like Miss Marilyn don't speak about."

"Jezebel's profession." I thought for a moment. "You know, with her name, it was as if she were set up."

"Well, that wasn't her name. She changed it."

"She did?"

"Why, yes. It was back before you were conceived." Miss Guidry peered at the doorway. "I don't suppose anyone else will tell you this, but your momma didn't choose to do what she did. That's why she did it differently than her momma. She was a real smart business lady." Miss Guidry nodded. "It was a new time. Women were making names for themselves. Her future was brighter than her momma's had been. Businesses were booming. New Orleans was on everyone's radar. That said, this city is old and doesn't always keep up with the times. I suppose your grandmother's story is an example of that. Heaven, selling off a daughter during those times...you'd think we were talking 1800s, not the mid-twentieth century."

"What business did my mother have?"

A smile spread across Miss Guidry's face. "Her dream was event planning. Now, she never went to school beyond high school, but she was a reader and, Lordy, she is great with figures. Back then, she had visions of what could be done in not only the French Quarter, but beyond. Her biggest obstacle was her name, North."

"So she chose Jezebel?"

"Yes, ma'am. It was her way of claiming her past and staking her future."

"What happened?"

Miss Guidry's smile disappeared. "In those days, nothing happened in New Orleans without the approval of the Ramseses or the Boudreaux. She made the wrong choice. When she went to Mr. Boudreau, he made her an offer."

My stomach turned at the way she said that. "A business deal?"

Miss Guidry looked around to be certain we were still alone. "You're wise enough to know what men want. Your momma refused. Well, Mr. Boudreau blackballed her. She'd gotten a small loan from the bank and they called it due. No one would give her the time of day. She went to Mr. Ramses, but he and Mr. Boudreau had an agreement."

"Rett's father wouldn't help her?"

"The two men, they had an understanding. After Mr. Boudreau shunned her, it was beyond Mr. Abraham to help. Your momma did what she could. Her options were limited. Event planning would never work. She knew the hotel owners and big venues wouldn't work with her. But she didn't give up."

"What did she do?"

Miss Guidry sat taller. "Jezebel went into a different business, the oldest profession, selling what was marketable."

I nodded. "I heard."

"Now, don't you be ashamed of a hardworking woman. She didn't do all the work. Some would call her a madam. She ran a right-nice escort service. She made money and learned how to invest it. Businessmen like to talk."

"Was that before or after I was born?"

"It started before."

"And she and Mr. Boudreau became partners in that business?" I asked.

Miss Guidry's eyes widened. "No."

"What happened?"

Miss Guidry looked down and wiped her hands on her apron. "Your mother would rather I don't say any more, specially not after what happened to you."

*What happened to me?*

Surely she didn't mean recently.

*Had Rett shared those details with Miss Guidry?*

I couldn't believe he had. Then again, my face was still bruised and my wrists and ankles still bandaged.

She forced a smile. "Just know, Miss Marilyn is—"

"Miss Guidry."

We both jumped at the volume and tone coming from the man in the doorway.

"Rett, we were just—"

He lifted his hand toward me as he continued staring at Miss Guidry.

Her lips came together and she stood. With a smile, she spoke to me. "Don't you never mind this old lady." She turned to Rett. "I was just fixin' to get the dessert." Her smile returned to me. "You deserved to know that your being here has made so many of us happy."

Warmth crept up my neck to my cheeks. "Thank you."

With barely another glance toward Rett, Miss Guidry hurried from the dining room.

Shaking his head, Rett took his seat. "Should I ask?"

"What happened between Isaiah Boudreau and Jezebel North? And what was her name before she changed it?"

Rett balled the cloth napkin he had half a second earlier placed over his leg and threw it on the table. "Christ, Emma." He motioned toward the door. "She's nuts. I should just insist she leave."

"No."

His stare met mine and his cadence slowed. "She speaks regularly to dead people."

"Just like that little boy in the movie."

"This isn't a movie, Emma. I've lived with this all my life. Now it's my mother. Before that it was my grandfather and grandmother."

"Why doesn't Miss Guidry speak of your father?" I asked.

"Because he's dead."

"So is your mother, or is she somewhere in this big house and you haven't told me."

Exhaling, Rett leaned back in his chair and buttoned his suit coat. "My mother—you've heard her name from Miss Guidry—was Marilyn Ramses. She passed away after my father. She and my father are in the family crypt. I assure you, she isn't here nor does she talk with Miss Guidry."

With Rett's obvious annoyance at the subject, I avoided it until we were back in my suite and the blindfold was gone.

"What does Miss Guidry or anyone else know about what happened to me—recently?"

It was the first time I'd mentioned it since the meeting in Rett's office with his men, successfully compartmentalizing the happenings away and concentrating on healing. Whenever memories surfaced, I made myself focus on something else. For over a week, it had worked.

Rett ran his thumb gently over my bruised cheekbone. Like my thoughts, my cheek was healing. No longer purple, it was a lovely shade of yellowish green, without makeup.

"She can see you, Emma." He lifted my hand, indicating the bandages. "Miss Guidry is crazy; she's not blind. She's also intuitive and some would say empathic. In my opinion, she mistakes her ability to sense the emotions of others with speaking to spirits."

"Did you tell her?"

He shook his head. "No. You told the men in my office."

The scene came back—me, Rett, Ian, and two other men. "Would they have told her?"

"No. My people understand discretion better than most."

I brought my lips together and walked to the window. The temperatures had cooled, not to a chilly degree but comfortable, and the humidity dropped. The window was open to the courtyard below. The fountain, a story below, was mesmerizing as its lights changed colors.

Rett came up behind me and wrapped his arms around my waist. "Talk, Emma."

I shrugged in his grasp before leaning my head back against his solid chest.

"What did she say?" he asked.

"It was more what she didn't say." I spun in his arms. "Don't be mad at her. She was excited to tell me that..." I hesitated. "...that your mother approves of me."

He scoffed. "She would, yes."

That simple comment shouldn't fill me with happiness, but it did.

"What didn't Miss Guidry say?" he asked again.

"I don't know. Something about my...Jezebel and Mr. Boudreau. I got a weird feeling that..." I wasn't sure how to phrase it.

Finally, Rett laid a kiss on my forehead and walked to the other side of the room. It was hard not to notice how nice he looked for our dinners. The suit he wore was not the one he'd worn all day. His cheeks were freshly shaven and he smelled divine. I was growing accustomed to his cologne.

"None of it matters," he said. "Don't overthink what

she says. When I was a boy, my friends called her Crazy Guidry."

A grin came to my lips. "You had friends?"

"Believe it or not. That was a long time ago. Before I sold my soul for what I have."

"To the devil?"

"To become the devil."

I walked over to him until we were close enough to touch. "I'll believe a lot of things about you, Rett Ramses. I won't believe that."

"No matter what Guidry tells you or what you learn, I want you to believe what I'm about to say." His gaze lowered to my neckline and back. "Believe this with all your heart, Emma. You are a queen." He cupped my cheeks. "This city is filled with stories, good versus evil. That ongoing battle becomes ingrained in our psyche from a young age. Not all good comes from good nor all bad comes from evil. Sometimes the opposite is true. Evil from good and good from evil. You are good."

His words settled over me.

"I need to do some work, Emma. Once this is over, we'll have more time together."

I sighed as he lifted my hand and kissed my knuckles.

Once more, he said, "Talk to me."

I was quickly learning it was one of his favorite phrases. Though I was hesitant, I voiced my thoughts. "What happened to the man in the restaurant, the one I woke to my first morning?"

Rett's grin returned. "He's waiting."

"For what?"

Rett gently ran his finger down my cheek. His touch continued down my arm until my hand was again in his. "You were conceived for me, to be my wife. What is happening here isn't a sprint. It is a marathon. I'm learning about you and you about me."

Keeping my lips together, I exhaled.

"And for you to heal, and..." His dark brown eyes glistened as he lifted my hand. "I'm waiting until you're ready to give me what I want."

*Submission.*

He kissed my knuckles again and turned toward his suite.

"I wear the stupid blindfold."

Rett turned back and grinned. "You do."

With a bow, he disappeared behind the door to his suite.

Letting out a long breath, I sat on the edge of the bed.

"I don't know what you want." Yes, I said it aloud, but he didn't hear me.

My thoughts returned to my conversation with Miss Guidry.

# EMMA

*I* spent the rest of my evening with thoughts of Jezebel and Isaiah. Two people I'd never met. I would guess that technically, I'd met Jezebel, but my memory of her didn't exist. I began wondering more about them.

*What did they look like?*

*Did I look like either of them?*

Another thought came to me in my musings; I began to think about Kyle. The information I'd received upon my parents' death was that *I* had been adopted. It had come in a file with the name Jezebel North.

*What about Kyle?*

According to Rett, he wasn't the biological son of Marcella and Oliver O'Brien. He too was adopted, but from who?

We were only separated in age by eight months. Our mother had said she'd been blessed with two children.

I'd assumed that I was born early or there was another medical explanation. Upon learning I'd been adopted, the age difference made more sense.

If only I had internet attached to the laptop Ian had retrieved from upstairs, I could search. I would look for pictures or stories. Rett was right about New Orleans and its perpetuation of lore. What I didn't know was how much of what I'd been told was truth and how much was fabricated or embellished.

Miss Guidry's story came back to me, clouding my mind, and making me unable to read the mystery I still hadn't finished. I went back to the manuscript I'd begun and read, wondering how much the sweet old woman was wearing off on me and how much was my imagination.

There was no doubt that Miss Guidry once had a close relationship with Marilyn Ramses. After all, it seemed as though she'd dedicated her life to be with Mrs. Ramses. As I was combing my hair before bed, my thoughts moved onto Jezebel, wondering what her name had been before she changed it, and wondering what it was like, as recently as twenty-six or more years ago, for a single woman, one who came from a sordid family history.

Since their death, I'd refused to devote the emotion I should to the people who raised me. Learning of their deceit, or maybe lack of transparency, had clouded the memories of my first twenty-two years.

All alone and staring down at the crest, I realized

how unfair I'd been to their memory. In reality, I'd been blessed with the O'Briens. They raised me to believe that I could do anything and everything that I set my mind to accomplish. They never pit me against Kyle or the other way around. I didn't grow up in competition with my brother or with the need to prove myself, as the female. Both Oliver and Marcella showed us that all anyone needed was hard work and devotion.

Maybe that was why I was willing to go into business with Ross. I'd refused to accept that my degree in literature would go unused.

It's odd how the mind worked.

One thought led to the next with no coherent path or safety net.

The breeze through the windows grew unseasonably cool. Instead of closing the panes, I wrapped the chenille robe over the satin shorts and camisole pajamas and sat across from the fireplace. Ian had shown me how to open a flue and push a button. It wasn't complicated and in seconds, I had a warm fire.

Watching the flames, my thoughts went to the woman who gave birth to me. From what Miss Guidry said, Jezebel wanted to be more than her mother was and to accomplish great things. Yet she didn't have the support of people like the O'Briens.

Even thirty years ago, she was held back by her gender and status. New Orleans was a different world, but I questioned if that were true. Misogyny hadn't disappeared. The decades had changed and yet the

Equal Rights Amendment to give all Americans equal rights regardless of gender that had been proposed in 1972 still wasn't the law of the land. The Constitution provided that amendments take effect when ratified by three-quarters of the states. That meant thirty-eight states. Nearly fifty years since it was proposed, the thirty-eighth state, Virginia, ratified the amendment.

That didn't mean it was law.

Half a century later, there were still hurdles that needed to be cleared to simply establish a legal standard of equality.

Were we still living in the world of my birth mother and her mother?

Did we simply hide it better, learning loopholes?

Had I gone into business with Ross, a known womanizer, because he was a man and that would somehow aid in our success?

*Was I like my mother who had gone to Isaiah Boudreau for help?*

Times had changed. Women had made headway. It was what I told myself as I lowered the flame and climbed in between the soft sheets. I never agreed with the way Ross handled women in romantic relationships, but he was my friend. I was complacent.

*Did that mean I'd condoned his behavior?*

*What happened to Jezebel?*

As I began to doze off, Miss Guidry's words came back to me. *"Your mother would rather I don't say any more, not after what happened to you."*

My heart ached as my imagination took a dark twist.

Jezebel wasn't in business with Isaiah Boudreau as I was in business with Ross Underwood. I doubted there was a financial agreement, the creation of a business entity, contracts, and shared bank accounts.

*"...after what happened to you."*

I had been taken and hurt.

I sat up in bed with the realization—Jezebel was hurt.

Maybe it was Miss Guidry and her talking to spirits, or maybe being in this house and city, my mother was talking to me, but as I began to fall asleep, I knew I was right. Jezebel North had been hurt, and she had been hurt by Isaiah Boudreau.

Rett's voice came to me. *"This city is filled with stories, good versus evil. It becomes ingrained in our psyche from a young age. Not all good comes from good nor all bad comes from evil. Sometimes the opposite is true. Evil from good and good from evil. You are good."*

Good can come from evil.

I came from Isaiah and Jezebel's union.

That union wasn't consensual.

Isaiah Boudreau had raped Jezebel.

It was a story of old, repeated through the centuries. A powerful man and the daughter of a whore, no one would believe her, and then the evidence became visible—me.

It was my last thought as sleep took over.

Over and over, I tossed and turned. My thoughts

were no longer on the parents I'd never met, but on the two men I never saw. They were right here, their voices, their smell, and their cruel words...

"Emma."

"Stop." I tried to fight, but I couldn't move. My hands and legs were bound. My heart beat faster, drumming against my breastbone. It didn't register that my name had been said. They hadn't said it before.

*Breathe, Emma, breathe.*

If I wasn't careful, I'd faint. No, I couldn't faint. I had to fight. I thrust my head from side to side.

"Emma, wake up."

My head continued to thrash as I fought. He was strong, yet I used my might and pushed him away.

*How could I push?*

"Emma, you're safe. You're safe."

My eyes sprang open. Unlike the room upstairs, in this suite illumination came through the windows, a combination of changing colors and hues with the moon's rays as well as the glow of the fire I'd left burning.

Scrambling toward the headboard, I lifted my arms and moved my feet. I wasn't tied to a chair. I was in my bed, the one I'd been told was mine. And I wasn't alone.

"Rett?"

The mountain of a man beside me wasn't my attacker. Before I could say more, he wrapped me in his arms, holding me hostage against his warm skin. His masculine scent filled my senses as his heart beat in double time beneath my ear.

"You are all right," he reassured.

I didn't want to let go of him as I wrapped my arms around his torso and kept my cheek against him.

Rett's hand moved in small circles on my back as his deep, comforting tone soothed the terror of the nightmare that had awakened me. "It was a dream. Just a dream."

"It seemed real. I heard them—the men."

"Lie back, Emma." He pushed me gently away. "Those men are dead. They can't hurt you."

Sighing, I laid my head back on the pillow. With the changing lights and warm orange glow, I could make out the definition in Rett's chest and torso. I saw the way the muscles in his arms bulged when he moved, the tightness in his jaw, and straining tendons in his neck.

He exemplified the persona he claimed. Everett Ramses was a ruler, a killer, and in his words, the devil. His harsh masculine beauty made him all the more dangerous, and yet he was here with me, reassuring me.

"You won't hurt me either."

The muscles on the side of his face grew taut. "Fuck, Emma."

"You won't. You say you're bad. If that's true, why are you here?"

"It's my house."

"Why are you *here*?"

"You were screaming."

I ran my hand over his arm. "I'm tired of waiting."

"You said you wanted to know more about me than my ability to make you orgasm."

"I know more about you." I quipped, "Remind me about the other part."

His eyes shut and his nostrils flared.

Scooting away, I made my way to the floor. With no real plan, I bent my knees and knelt at the side of the bed. My hands shook as I wondered where they were supposed to be. "Rett, I confess, I have no idea what I'm doing."

He smiled.

Sitting back on my knees and bent toes, I went on, "But I want to give you what you want."

Rett turned until his bare feet were on the floor, spaced in front of me. It was then I noticed his legs. It was an odd observation, but never before had I seen him without long pants. As I scanned I realized that even his calves and thighs were muscular. There wasn't anything about Everett Ramses that wasn't sexy.

He leaned down, placed one finger under my chin, and held it higher. "Tell me what you want, Emma."

"I did."

"You know what I want." It wasn't a question.

I nodded as my lip disappeared between my teeth.

"Talk to me."

I was honest. "I'm scared."

"No, you're not. This right here and right now isn't frightening. You've been through much worse, and you're the bravest woman I know. Admit to yourself and to me what this does feel like. It's like the night I met you at the restaurant, Emma. It's not fear. It's exhilaration. It's stimulating."

His observation fit.

I was feeling a myriad of emotions. There was part that was new and intriguing, but there was also fear. "You're right, but so am I. I'm scared that I'll not be who you want or in the process, I'll lose me. You want me to be weak and I'm not."

Rett offered me his hand. Seeing his outstretched palm, I sighed, struck by the realization that I'd tried and failed.

It was as I stood that Rett spoke. "I don't want you weak. I never said that." He tugged me between his knees. His only clothing was a pair of silk boxer briefs that even in the darkness left little to the imagination.

"Then I don't understand."

Rett eased me up onto one of his legs and lifted my legs until I was across his lap. His erection twitched beneath me, yet his words were less erotic and more educational. "The night I brought you home, after you were taken..."

I nodded again.

"Do you remember what you called me, what you said I was?"

My hand rested on his chest. "I said you were nice."

"After the few weeks you've been with me, do you think nice is easy for me?"

"I mean, mostly...but that night you were also upset."

"I was furious."

"But you were still nice," I said.

"Because if I'd reacted toward you as I had Ian or the others I'd blamed for your stupid move, I would have terrified you. You were already traumatized. I restrained my anger because you needed that. One night doesn't make me a nice person. It also doesn't make me a fake or weak. It took fucking more restraint to carry you up here and play nice with Dr. Dustin than it would have to bark orders and break things or punch walls.

"I was able to be nice because I'm not weak. I'm in control. That's what I want from you." He ran his finger down my cheek. "You're fucking strong, Emma. You threatened to bite off dicks." He grinned. "Submission from a weak woman doesn't do it for me. It's like fucking a scared puppy. From the moment you resisted going into Broussard's with me, I knew what I wanted. I want you to submit to me because I know in here" —he laid his hand over my breasts— "you are the polar opposite of submissive."

"So you want me to not be me?"

"No, I want you to be you, going against your instincts because you want to please me. When you can do that, I promise you, I won't see you as weak. I won't lose the admiration I have. It'll grow because I see your conflict and your ability to rein it in. The first night I told you that I'd bring you pleasure and pain. The pain is in here." He touched my temple. "It's a battle that you will fight. It's like the blindfolds, the way you hated them at first."

"You knew that?"

"I loved that. I'd think about you, the way you submitted but how it made you bristle." He scoffed. "I'd have to think about killing someone to make my cock go down. The thoughts of you made me hard."

"I'm used to the blindfolds."

"Then take it another step."

I shook my head. "I tried and you didn't..."

"Let me help you, Emma, and those orgasms you had the first two days will be minor tremors compared to the earthquakes we'll find together."

I didn't respond, not because I was confused. On the contrary, what Rett said made sense.

He lifted my chin. "Why haven't you come to my suite?"

"Because you haven't asked me."

He stood, helping me to my feet. "Something you should know about me. I don't ask."

I straightened my neck and my nipples grew taut as I inhaled.

"Follow me to my suite."

"Do you want me?"

I let out a sigh as Rett tilted my head forward and kissed my hair. His cadence was measured, yet his tone had dropped an octave. "I've wanted you since the first time I saw you and your haunting blue eyes. A minute hasn't passed that I haven't imagined being inside you."

I squeezed my thighs, as with only words, this man could melt my core. My breasts throbbed as my nipples went from hard to diamond and deep inside of me, my pussy clenched with need. Without another word, Rett turned toward the door to his suite and began to walk.

I reeled, wondering what had happened.

*Shouldn't he reach out or tug me along?*

*Did he expect me to follow?*

*What if I did and he rejected me again?*

When Rett reached the door, he opened it. Without turning back, he said, "On your hands and knees."

My breath caught as my eyes opened wide.

Leaving the door open, he disappeared into the darkness.

# RETT

*I* wasn't confident of Emma's next move as I left her suite. I was confident in almost every other facet of my life, my past decisions, my future choices, and my lasting reign over New Orleans. My fuse could be short or it could be painstakingly long. I dubbed knights in my army and declared generals, granting them the power to do my bidding. I'd taken lives without blinking an eye, seized property and wealth. I'd also had my share of women.

My tastes were too much for some and not enough for others. Whether I was easing my hard cock into a tight pussy or fucking ruby-red lips, both worked for me. What I didn't do, hadn't done, was take the time to learn more than the physical pleasure I could receive. I'd never been a selfish lover—the term *lover* not meant to insinuate emotion—since there was no reason I couldn't bring pleasure as I found release. In a nutshell, fucking relieved pent-up energy.

It was beyond the physical that I'd never wanted.

Staying true to course had been my intention with Emma.

Fate had destined our union, and I'd fucking tempted fate too many times to not give in on this one. All it took was one look at her soft curves, haunting blue eyes, and luscious golden crown of hair, and I knew I'd keep her. From the moment our eyes met, she was mine. The night at the restaurant I moved fast, anxious to learn if she was as delicious on the inside as she was to the eyes.

Maybe there was another goal, to scare her away.

If I were a man who experienced fear, it would have been me who left that night trembling. Emma's receptiveness and exhilaration combined with a hefty dose of apprehension had me intoxicated.

I told myself that night was the last time I'd touch her like that until she proved herself.

That next morning, I went against my own decree. Emma had been asleep so long. I'd gotten hard watching her pert parted lips and the noises she'd made in her sleep.

One more time.

It was the agreement I'd made with myself.

One more time to hear her cries of pleasure, to taste her sweet essence, and to feel the softness of her skin. I was a man of my word.

Since that morning, I'd spent more time jacking off than I cared to admit, even to myself.

But until tonight, telling Emma to follow, I'd kept my word.

The day she'd dared to leave, my obsession to bring her pleasure morphed into one to bring her true pain, to punish her, and to make her pay for the consequences of her actions. I'd considered a bullet. It wasn't a thought I was proud to admit, but it had come to me. And then there she was, tied to that chair in that god-awful den, and in her fear and confusion, she'd called for me. With her eyes blindfolded and blood splattered over her skin, she called my name.

Emma North had her mother's power of enticement. She also had her father's spirit and determination. What I wondered as I lit the fire in my fireplace was if she had what it took to be my wife. She would be. That was set.

That role would either be her death or bring her life.

The orange flames coated my suite, leaving the corners in shadows of the unknown. My private area covered multiple rooms. Years ago, it had been my father's, before him, my grandfather's, and further back up the paternal line of Ramses men. From stories I'd heard, they'd all bedded mistresses while their wives slept a short hallway and room away.

That wasn't my style.

In the eight years since I took control of New Orleans, no woman had entered this suite for my sexual pleasure. Taking a deep breath, I turned toward the small hallway connecting our suites. My chest tightened as the floor squeaked. The barely audible noise was like fucking music. I stepped back into the shadows with the knowledge that Emma had followed.

Still upright and emerging from the dark hallway, Emma's eyes opened wide as she took in the grandeur my grandfather had commissioned. She couldn't see me and didn't know she was being watched.

Indecision showed on her beautiful face as she took one small step and then another. Still standing, she scanned the room, searching its depths. Like a sheep to the slaughter, she moved forward, her head high and her eyes filled with curiosity.

Had she expected a Saint Andrew's cross or a wall lined with crops and whips?

That wasn't what I sought from her, or from anyone.

The submission I craved took more strength than accepting the bite of an implement.

What I wanted was what was happening in front of me. My cock grew painfully hard as Emma's breasts heaved beneath the silk top and she slowly made her way into the main room. She turned slowly, making a complete circle as she stared at the walls.

My great-grandfather had a fascination with the darker side of New Orleans. The large pieces of artwork in heavy golden frames displayed depictions of Hades, the underworld, a world of torment and pain. Much like a story, the pieces went together, displaying the battles beyond the realm where most people reside. According to the artist, that war continues. One battle may be won or lost, depending if it is good or evil that you root for. The impressionist style and use of colors makes the scenes difficult to decipher.

If my grandfather hadn't passed the story and each frame's meanings onto me through his journals, I might not see what was right before me. That's the way it was with the beliefs held by many in this region. They saw what others didn't.

Honestly, I rarely gave the art any thought, but seeing them through her angelic eyes was fascinating to watch.

Finally, Emma's legs bent and she lowered herself to the hard floor. She was fucking gorgeous as she made her way to her knees. Emma hadn't entered on her hands and knees, but as I watched her internal battle, her willpower surrendered to her exhilaration and she submitted.

I remained silent, letting Emma wait as she sat back on her heels, lowering her chin.

My response was in my thoughts. "Good girl, but that wasn't what I told you."

With the light of the fire, Emma glowed like the queen she was meant to be. Queens weren't meant to bow except to one person. Once it was safe to display her to the world, she wouldn't show them what I was seeing—what only I would see. Out in the world, she'd hold her head high as Emma Ramses. Her submission was for me and me alone.

My cock ached as it pressed against my boxer briefs, straining the expensive threads.

As if Emma suddenly remembered my final command, she fell forward, placing her palms on the floor and her sexy round ass in the air. If I wasn't so fucking ready to be inside her, I'd use this opportunity to teach her about patience. The way her knees fidgeted, her body was ready to find out what came next even if her mind was conflicted.

I took a step forward out of the shadows.

"Oh," she startled before dropping her head.

Without a word, I stepped around her, circling her like the predator I was. The way a lion played with his prey, I continued my slow steps. Her long golden hair covered her face, her arms trembled, and her breathing was fast.

One finger, it was all I would use to move her.

I'd sensed her receptiveness when I'd directed her blindfolded. A little pressure and she obeyed. Emma didn't think she was submissive. I wanted her to learn it was nothing to be ashamed of, but instead, something she enjoyed.

I crouched before her and placed my finger under her chin. Very little pressure and her gorgeous blue eyes appeared. They lingered on my confined erection before making the journey upward to my gaze.

"You're stunning."

Her lip disappeared behind her teeth, the way it did when she was thinking. I tugged it free. "No, Emma, don't overthink this."

"I..." Her eyes widened and tone softened. "May I speak?"

I was going to fucking blow in a second.

"Always. Sit back."

She did, sitting back on her heels. Her hard nipples tented her silk top and with the way her knees were parted, the crotch of the silky shorts showed signs of her wetness. I was still crouched down, our faces inches apart.

"Talk."

"Will you tell me if I'm doing this wrong?"

I shook my head.

"How will I know if I disappoint you?"

Reaching for the hem of her top, I slowly pulled it over her head. As I dropped the silk to the floor, her blonde hair cascaded around her shoulders. Emma's gaze was on me, waiting for my answer. My answer was that she couldn't disappoint me. She'd upset me and I'd upset her. It was the way relationships worked.

But disappoint?

I ran my hands down her arms. Stopping at her wrists, I took in the bandages. They were smaller than they'd been a week before. I couldn't concentrate on that. Taking both her hands, I lifted her arms above her head. It wasn't an easy position to maintain. Yet when I let go, she kept them raised. A soft moan came from her lips as my finger ran down her inner arm.

With her hands held high, her round breasts thrust forward. Her nipples grew even harder as I tweaked one and then the other. My gaze didn't leave hers as I rolled one between my fingers. Her eyes fluttered closed as her breathing staggered. I pinched harder. "Eyes open, Emma."

Blues like the shades of a churning ocean filled my view.

"You won't disappoint me."

A small smile brought turquoise calm to the churning sea.

Without another word, I stood and offered her my hand.

With her palm in mine, I sensed a slight tremble of insecurity. That emotion wasn't alone. I also felt her excitement as I took her to the large rug in front of the fireplace. Tugging on her silky shorts, I pulled them down her shapely legs until she was standing completely nude. I walked around her, then eased her long locks behind her shoulders to expose her round breasts.

Her red nipples displayed the evidence of my earlier attention.

It was the first time I'd seen her, all of her. In the past, I'd compared Emma to a fine wine, but seeing her standing in front of me, she was more. Emma North was a goddamned masterpiece created for me. No sculptor could create the perfectly placed planes, mounds, and curves. I couldn't look away from her faultlessness.

"Spread your legs."

A shiver washed over her as she obeyed.

Taking a step back, I saw the way the firelight reflected off her inner thighs, more evidence of her arousal. The goose bumps gracing her soft alabaster skin weren't from the temperature. On the contrary, the fireplace opening was nearly her height, the flames crackling within radiating heat.

"Kneel for me, like you were, on your heels."

With the grace of a gazelle, Emma folded her body, bending one leg and then the other, keeping her blue gaze set on me.

"You won't leave this room without pleasure. First, I'm going to make you wait."

Her eyes opened wider.

"It's my turn."

Her breathing quickened and her pink tongue darted to her lips. If it wasn't the sexiest thing I'd ever seen... I'd had meetings and gatherings where women and men flaunted their attributes while grinding to music in what many considered lewd and crude performances. Not one of those exhibitions ever did for me what Emma was doing right now.

Pushing down my boxer briefs, I freed my hard cock.

"Do you know what I want?"

Emma nodded. "You want me to suck you."

Come glistened on the tip of my penis.

"What do you want?"

Her neck and spine straightened. "I want that too."

"Don't open your mouth."

Using my cock like a giant tube of lipstick, I painted her pink lips. Her eyes closed as I covered her lips in my gloss. "Lick it."

Emma didn't hesitate, her tongue winding all around like a kitten who'd just finished her saucer of milk. Her eyes widened as she stared up and waited for my commands. "Hands behind your back and mouth open."

Fuck, her soft lips and warm mouth were almost too much.

I hadn't worked this hard for this long to blow my load in seconds. My feet spread apart as she took me as far as she could, bobbing her head. It was heaven and fucking hell all rolled into one. My mind was so wrapped up in her amazing mouth that I hadn't noticed how she'd moved, sitting upward with her petite hands on my thighs.

The rush within me built fast.

I weaved my fingers in her long hair as my hips pistoned against her. The suite filled with my rapid breaths and Emma's mews. I began to pull out, reminding myself that this woman was my fucking queen, not a whore, but her hands had moved again, gripping the back of my thighs. Looking down, I was mesmerized, lost in her pose and poise.

Emma was a queen with the regal touch of a whore.

No longer holding back, I came, waiting for her to complain.

Instead, she finished me. Once she was done, I offered her my hand.

As she stood, I pulled her close. "God, Emma, don't ever ask me if you disappoint me. You're perfect."

## EMMA

*T*wo words—you're perfect.

My sore knees and strained jaw disappeared. I could bask in the shine of Rett's brown eyes for longer than I cared to admit. Before I could give that startling new realization much thought, my feet left the floor. Cradled in Rett's strong arms, he carried me to the large bed, threw back the blankets and laid me on the sheets.

I'd never seen a bed as massive as the one in his suite.

If I were honest, his whole suite was intimidating.

It dwarfed me.

The framed artwork was gigantic, and the odd paintings gave me an uncomfortable feeling, the fireplace was taller than I was, and truly all of the furnishings were imposing. When I'd entered, I had the strange sensation that I'd shrunk or the world around me had gotten bigger.

Before I gave the room around me any more thought, Rett was over me, his nose touching mine, and his still-hard rod poised at my core.

Nothing else mattered as his dark eyes stared into mine.

My mind and body were consumed with the here and now.

Moments before were lost. Even the promise I'd made to submit was forgotten. Every thought was consumed with what Rett was doing, the way his touch skirted over me, searching and claiming, how his forceful firm lips took mine, and the way his tongue unapologetically sought mine.

I lifted my hips as I imagined the large cock I'd had in my mouth, deep inside me.

Rett's deep baritone tenor filled the air with praises as kisses and nips covered my skin. His touch moved lower until his warm breath teased my sensitive skin. There was no doubt he was capable of bringing me pleasure with his talented lips and tongue, but I wanted him inside me, as he'd never been.

I reached for his cheeks, pulling him over me. "Please, Rett." His penetrating gaze met mine. "I want you—just as you were saying—inside me."

"There's no fighting this."

"I'm not fighting."

His stare swirled with emotions he wasn't saying.

They were too numerous to read or maybe I was too inexperienced with a man as complicated as Everett Ramses to understand. Truth was my only option. I wasn't certain I was capable of lying to him even if I wanted to, not the way he looked at me, saw me, as if he could see inside my mind.

"Rett, please."

Settling between my bent legs his nose came back to mine. "You're mine."

That revelation had been told to me at our first meeting. Even then, as outrageous as it sounded, I had no reason to doubt it. That said, I'd never believed it as much as I did at this moment. "I am."

"Say it, Emma."

"I'm yours, Rett."

Pushing my knees back, he stared down at me. "This pussy is fucking mine. Anyone else sees it or touches it, they'll die by my hand."

I nodded.

Rett wouldn't be my first, but I was beginning to comprehend the reach of his power. As long as he wanted me, I would be his. Once we came together, there would be no changing my mind. The only way I'd escape this man's grasp would be death.

To some people that would seem a frightening realization.

Maybe three weeks ago it would have sent me packing. Too much had happened since the night I first saw him across the restaurant. Whether here in his bed or across a table filled with delicacies, Rett's penetrating gaze took my breath away. Having his attention intoxicated me. The tenor and command in his voice left me spellbound, and his touch over my skin or his lips on mine was a drug I quickly found addicting.

The comprehension that this act would be our unbreakable connection didn't scare me. It filled me with anticipation for what life with him would be. Rett's protective ways gave me safety. His proprietary words gave me the freedom to try. And his need for submission gave me strength.

The contradictory feelings weren't lost on me, but they also couldn't be denied.

He sat back. "Get back on your hands and knees, Emma."

My heart fluttered a bit as I moved as he'd said. Somewhere in my mind, I'd expected our first encounter to be normal. What had Rett said? Normal was ordinary. There was nothing ordinary about the man holding my hips, positioning me, and about to take me.

Everett Ramses lived life hard. He took what he wanted without apology.

Two fingers found my core.

"You're soaked."

"It's you."

It was. I couldn't explain it. I wasn't under an illusion that Rett and I were madly in love. I'd told him upfront that he'd never have my heart. This wasn't a make-believe fairy tale where he was Prince Charming and I was some damsel in distress. Before Rett had entered my life, I was competent and content.

And yet before meeting him, I didn't know that my body could or would react the way it did with him. Never before had anyone had that effect. Under his touch I was putty and Everett Ramses was the sculptor.

I stretched my neck, my back arching, as his fingers worked me, priming me and taking my mind away from anything but his touch. There was no warning as his fingers disappeared and he plunged deep inside me. No easing in. No slow burn. In seconds, he was balls deep.

The feeling of fullness was overwhelming, knocking me forward.

I struggled to resume my position as Rett gripped my hips, holding me captive in his grasp. I was lost in the rhythm he created as our bodies slapped against one another. The room with the massive furniture was no longer present.

We could have been in my suite or in the middle of Bourbon Street. Thinking beyond us—this—was impossible. Never in my life had I been taken so thoroughly. Rett pressed down on my shoulders until only my ass stayed in the air. The slight change was electric. I struggled to breathe against the pillows as synapses fired and shocks detonated. It was as he reached around and rolled my clit between his fingers that I exploded, a massive earthquake registering off the Richter scale.

I called out his name as aftershocks ricocheted through my body.

Rett didn't stop or even slow as I fought to remain upright.

My scalp cried out as he wound his fingers through my hair, pulling my head backward. I had the sensation of a cowboy riding a wild mare. I was the mare, my body bucking beyond my own doing. It was an out-of-body experience with the perks of feeling every sensation. I was here and I was above. I heard Rett's straining breaths and felt the power of his thrusts. My second orgasm hit me like a freight train seconds before the room filled with Rett's primal roar and he filled me.

I fell to the sheets as he throbbed within me.

As Rett pulled out and rolled me over, I had things I wanted to say and questions I wanted to ask. Each one was lost to the overwhelming satiation that could only come from what had just happened.

Ready to sleep for days on end, I opened my eyes as Rett's handsome face appeared in my line of vision. His dark hair hung near his face, disheveled by his recent physical endeavor. I wanted to reach up to rake my fingers through his wavy mane. Instead, I gripped the silky sheets as Rett was again inside me. Soft kisses covered my face, neck, and collarbone, coming in sync with his new, slower rhythm. Releasing the sheets, I reached up, holding his wide shoulders as his striking brown stare met mine.

Our story continued in the dark waves of unspoken

emotion swirling in his chocolate orbs. I was lost to his ministrations.

My tired body responded much like a boat upon waves. Slow and steady. Up and down. Long lazy thrusts, deep inside and almost out. Each time I almost lost him, my body clamped down, not wanting to let Rett go.

In this position, I was keenly aware of Rett's skin against mine. It had been one of my thoughts, our lack of protection. I couldn't think about it now. My mind was consumed. His touch was electric as it roamed over and through me, fulfilling every need I'd never known I could have.

If what we'd done at first was the Rett the world knew, then this new calmer union was him showing me a glimpse of the man behind the facade. I couldn't say that one was better than the other. Deep down, I knew that a life with Everett Ramses would give me both.

His nose met mine. "You feel so fucking good."

My back arched, pressing my breasts against his hard chest. "I do."

This time when the orgasm came, it rumbled through me like the slow roll of thunder over the open plains. My fingers blanched on his shoulders as I held on, impervious to anything beyond the bubble we'd created.

In his arms, I fell asleep, sedated and satisfied, safe from the storms on the horizon.

# RETT

*N*odding to Henri, I stepped through the threshold to the sitting room of my front office. As Henri closed the large door behind me, my concentration was on the man currently in the process of standing. This time his presence wasn't a surprise. This meeting was overdue.

Afternoon sunlight streamed through the fifteen-foot windows as I moved forward.

"Everett," Richard Michelson said as he stood and extended his hand.

Taking his hand and giving it a quick shake, I nodded before taking the seat beside him. The aroma of the flowers on the table between us was overpowering. I'd ask Miss Guidry to trade them for something less fragrant once this meeting was over.

"I've been meaning to get back to you," Michelson said, resuming his seat.

Taking a breath, I leaned against the antique chair and released the button on my suit coat. "I expected this situation to be cleared up much sooner."

"It has barely been a month. You know there's a shitload of bureaucracy that requires time. I told you it was a new member on the force—"

I lifted my hand. "Honestly, Richard, I don't give a shit what it took or takes. Don't bore me with the hows or excuses on the whys. I called you here today to have you tell me that it's settled. From what I've heard, all the evidence is pointing toward suicide."

Michelson stood and paced a small trek over the Persian rug. That simple piece of floor covering cost more than Michelson made in two years on his prosecutor salary. It was also nearly as old as me. Watching his worn brown loafers go back and forth was wearing on my nerves.

He nodded, definitive nods, the kind people made when they weren't comfortable with their answer. "You see, it *is* settled...well, almost."

I motioned toward the chair. "Richard, sit. This isn't an inquisition. I would simply like to understand your definition of *is* and *almost*."

Instead of sitting, Michelson walked to one of the large windows and peered out onto the gardens beside my home. "Remember," he said, "when I mentioned a legal filing I'd helped with when I first started practicing law?" On the final word, he turned back.

"I recall you saying something about an old story from around the time when you were fresh out of law school." I lifted my eyebrows. "How long ago would that be?"

I anticipated the answer. It was twenty-six years ago, Emma's age.

"It seems like a lifetime. I suppose it was." Michelson's head shook as he resumed his seat. "Everett, I can't tell you more." His gray eyes looked up. "I want to. I can't."

"Why can't you?"

"The Underwood case is about wrapped up. There was another woman; her name was very close to Underwood's business partner...Oberyn. There's still no sign of the O'Brien woman. Oberyn's alibi during the time in question has been verified. The thing is, Everett, she and Underwood had a history. Hell, he wouldn't be the first man to pop some extra pills because of heartbreak."

It hadn't been my go-to story, but if it worked...

Richard continued, leaning forward with his elbows on his knees and his voice filled with concern. "The weird thing is that Underwood had an influx of cash from an undetermined off-shore account deposited into his account the morning before he arrived in New Orleans."

That wasn't news to me. I'd authorized the transfer. "Any idea where it came from?"

"Our guys have been searching, but so far, we're coming up empty. In reality, it isn't our biggest concern."

My eyebrows rose. "Then why mention it?"

"You see, the homicide department has this new guy —woman actually. She spent over ten years in Atlanta working cybercrime. Her aspiration is the feds. You could say she is more forward thinking." He looked up. "What do you know about cryptocurrency?"

I scoffed. I knew more than I wanted to share but less than I could explain. "Richard, if you're going to give me a test, you could have at least given me some time to study."

Michelson was out of the chair again. "That's the thing. Hell, we may never find the source of the off-shore deposit. We know it came from a shell company out of Switzerland via the Caymans. There are numerous shell companies. It probably can be traced back to Delaware. They really need to do something about the ease of shell..."

He waved his hand. In the sunlight, I saw how the stress he was under showed in his expression, the furrowed brow and lines at the corners of his eyes.

"If it weren't for my family," he said, "I'd personally do a tour of all the places that money bounced around. I could use a vacation."

"The cryptocurrency?" I asked.

"Our new lady figured out that Underwood had a Kraken account and has been receiving influxes of

Bitcoin for roughly eighteen months. The currency has sat untouched, and in today's market, it has grown exponentially. Now he and Emma O'Brien had a startup company—literature, editing, hell, I don't know. Anyway, according to everything we've seen, the two of them were in the market for investors." His head shook. "It doesn't make sense. Hell, Underwood could have subsidized the entire thing, and then let it die for a nice tax write-off. Maybe that was his plan."

"He had the money to support the company on his own?" I asked.

"What if Miss O'Brien figured it out?" Richard asked. "What if she realized he was using her to watch her fall?"

"Do you know that he was doing that for certain?"

"No. But it's a motive."

"A motive? I thought you no longer had her as a suspect?" I asked.

His head shook. "Officially, Everett, she isn't. The i's are getting dotted and t's crossed. By the end of the week, Underwood's death will be ruled a suicide. But fuck, it opens the door to more questions. His parents have already hired an attorney. And there's still the missing Miss Emma O'Brien."

Richard let out an exaggerated breath and sat again.

"Is there any way to learn who was depositing Bitcoin in Underwood's Kraken account?" It was a genuine question. As soon as this meeting was over, I would be on the phone with my people to find out how they missed this and what they could learn.

"Most cryptocurrency is associated with number codes. Hell, Everett, it's all Greek to me. The new girl, she brought me something that made me decide I should see you again, so when you called for this meeting, I knew I needed to tell you what I know." Perspiration dotted his brow, glistening in the sunshine from the window.

"Richard, are you well?"

He reached for a small notebook from his suit coat's inside pocket. As he thumbed the pages, I thought about the contrast in an old-fashioned notebook and discussing one of the newest forms of currency.

"Here it is." Michelson took a deep breath and began to read. "K-1-21112-135121111820."

"Is that supposed to mean something?"

"She explained it to me like this: if you take our alphabet and number each letter—A is one and so on— that number combination would spell Baal Melkart." When I didn't respond, he went on, "Baal refers to god or lord. The reference is to a biblical story from 1 Kings —thus the K and one. Baal Melkart was the Tyrian god of nature. Remember, the people of Phoenicia were not monotheistic but rather worshippers of many gods and goddesses."

My mind was searching desperately through Sunday school lessons from over thirty-five years ago. "First

Kings? It's been a while since I heard my mother's daily devotionals, Richard."

"You might recall the story, the daughter of the priest-king Ethbaal. He was the ruler of the Phoenician cities Tyre and Sidon."

Tyre and Sidon were ancient names of current regions.

I stood. "Why are we discussing Lebanon?"

"Who was the daughter of the priest-king, Everett? She was sent to Israel to marry King Ahab."

The answer sent a cold chill down my spine. "Jezebel."

Richard nodded. "Listen, I got along well with your father and Isaiah Boudreau. Things change. I've been as loyal to you as I can and still keep my job. I'm not deaf and neither are others in the department. Hell, we've even fielded some calls from the feds."

"What are you saying?" I asked as I stood taller, easily seven inches over Richard Michelson.

"I'm saying that it's been *almost* eight years since Abraham and Isaiah died. Call it New Orleans superstition, but sevens are significant. You know as well as I do that there's been rumblings of discontent in the greater parishes. This city was divided into Ramses and Boudreau. There are still those who had their allegiance with Isaiah and are willing to entertain stories of a Boudreau return."

"You've been watching too many ghost stories, Richard. The dead stay dead."

"I think that there's a plot underfoot. Emma O'Brien came to New Orleans either knowingly or unknowingly to stake a claim on her heritage. That deal I brokered, it was an adoption. I think someone paid Underwood to get Miss O'Brien here. Not only to get her here, but to keep her busy until the time was right."

"In cryptocurrency?" I was trying to keep his story straight. I hadn't used cryptocurrency. Hell, I hadn't even contacted Underwood until a few months ago. "When did Underwood begin receiving the Bitcoin deposits?"

"Around eighteen months ago."

"And there's no way to trace it?" I asked.

"The feds want to nose around. They don't give a shit about Underwood, but he opened the door. Suicide will stick, but if they have their druthers, those boys can get nosy. This talk of Boudreau could come back to you, Everett. You're Abraham's only child, only son. No one questioned you taking over what had been in your family.

"I remember when this went down. The whole damn city knew Miss North was with child," he continued. "They also knew who the father was." He shook his head. "I doubt some literature major with computer savvy came to New Orleans to take your place. I think she's a pawn in someone else's game."

"Are you saying that this Emma O'Brien is that child?"

"We really need to talk to her if you have any idea where she went."

"Last time you were here," I said, "you told me she was dangerous."

"We've learned a few things."

"What do you want to talk to her about, Richard?"

"That's really not your business."

Fuck that. Emma was my business. "Yet you came to me," I said. "That sure as fuck sounds like it's my business."

"First, we want to be sure she's alive. She's fallen off the radar—the grid—we haven't been able to find her. There's been nothing since the night she arrived. It's been over a month. My gut tells me that she is being hidden or" —he shook his head— "she didn't make it out of New Orleans alive." He reached into his pocket and pulled out a photograph. "Look at her, Everett. This is who we're discussing."

She's fucking stunning.

"She's a lovely woman."

Michelson stared a little longer at Emma's picture than I appreciated. He looked up with only his gray eyes. "She looks like her mother."

"You're certain this woman is Jezebel North's daughter?"

He stared down at the picture for a few more seconds and exhaled. "I'm worried about the girl. I'm afraid of who's using her. It's a dangerous game and it seems the generations of Ramseses and Boudreaux sharing power disappeared nearly eight years ago—still within the seventh year."

"Isaiah didn't have an heir to make a claim."

Richard shook his head. "This needs to stop now or it will be out of my hands, and I can't promise what will happen."

# EMMA

*I* stared at Rett in shock. His emotions were unreadable. The ring in my hand was heavy, a filigree platinum band with a giant oval diamond. I still couldn't believe what he'd just said.

"I need to marry you now. Tonight?"

Rett nodded. "I called in a few favors. The judge will be here in half an hour."

My head spun with this newfound urgency as I walked to the window in my suite that looked out on the courtyard. Though it was daylight, now that I'd seen it in the lights, I couldn't look down without seeing the Ramses family crest.

"Talk to me."

I spun back toward him. "Hell, Rett, I don't know what to say. I suppose somewhere in my head I'd imagined a man on his knee professing his love and extolling the reasons why we were meant to be husband

and wife." I tossed the ring in the air, just inches above my palm and then closed my fingers around it. "Having a dead woman's ring handed to me, being told that I was getting married in the next hour, and to be ready has honestly paled."

"It's a family heirloom. Some people find those sentimental."

I looked down at the ring. Though it was large for my taste, it was beautiful. "It was your grandmother's?"

"Yes, fuck, Emma. I'll make it up to you." Rett snatched the ring from my hand and fell to one knee. "Marry me."

My eyes closed as I turned away. My change of scenery didn't last long as my shoulders were seized, I was spun back toward Everett Ramses, and my eyes opened. "Maybe the third time will be the charm."

Rett ran his hand down his face. "This isn't about professing love. We both agreed to that from the beginning. I'm not a man capable of love. I gave that up when I took over this city. Love and what I do, what I've done, don't make good bedfellows."

There was a flicker of pain in his dark gaze.

"If I could love," he went on, "I would try with you, for you. Emotions aren't what matter at the end of the day. What matters is fulfilling fate's destiny. You, Emma, were created for this, for me, for us, and for New Orleans. There are some things I haven't mentioned, but the end result is that before we can make our deal public, before I can introduce you to the world, you may need to answer some questions, legal questions."

Rett was right about our agreement. I'd given my heart at too young of an age to a boy who left it shattered before leaving me in my time of need. The remaining shreds were all I had. I held on to them tight to keep my heart beating. I didn't have enough to share.

Inhaling, I lifted my chin. "Fine, love is off the table. Your reasoning for this new dire schedule is that I'm wanted for questioning? How is that possible? Who knows I'm here? Questioning about what?" A thought occurred to me. "It's you." My eyes opened wide. "You're concerned that I've learned too much about you and if we're married I can't testify against you. What is going on, Rett?"

Cupping my cheeks, he pulled my lips to his. Firm and strong, they stole my questions, my argument, and my protest. When Rett pulled back, we were nose to nose. "This was always our deal. You agreed to marry me."

My shoulders sagged as I looked up at him. "I did."

The too-handsome man before me reached for my hands, planting soft kisses to the faint pink lines around my wrists. The bandages were gone—the abduction and rescue a month ago—but Dr. Dustin said it would take time for the scars to fully fade.

"Emma, we don't need some Hallmark rendition of what marriage is about. And this isn't simply a business deal to unite our family names. Fuck, since you came into my life, I've become obsessed, not only with your safety. It's you. You're on my mind when I fall asleep and when I open my eyes. I think about you during the day, anxious to find you ready for dinner or reading in the sunlight. If you're not beside me in my bed, I feel the need to come in here and just watch you."

"Watch me?"

"Did you know you snore?"

"I do not."

"It's soft and your lips part enough that it takes all my willpower not to lean in and kiss them. And when I wake and you are there, I can't stop myself from slipping inside you and nudging you awake as you come apart."

My lips curled upward as warmth filled my cheeks. "I like that."

"There aren't any surprises here. You made a deal with the devil, and now it's time to sign on the dotted line. In an hour or less, you'll be Mrs. Everett Ramses."

I lifted one eyebrow as I shook my head. "No, I won't. Assuming I do this, I will be Mrs. Emma Ramses. Hell, why do I need to change my name? Maybe I could change O'Brien legally to North."

Snaking one arm around my waist, Rett pulled my hips to his. "I'm hard just thinking about this morning's wake-up call." His hands went to my waist as he lifted me to the window's ledge. Gathering the long gauze skirt and bringing it higher, he grinned. "And tomorrow's and the day after that."

I pushed against his strong chest, yet he didn't budge.

"I want you right now, Mrs. Emma Ramses. And in the morning, that will be your name because you're fucking taking mine. That isn't up for discussion."

"You're bossy."

"Only when I want my way."

A grin came to my lips. "I've noticed that." I held the skirt, stopping his progress before I was fully exposed. "That, what you said, it was a better proposal. Will you add the bended knee part?"

Once again, Rett was on one knee, his brown eyes seeing only me. "Give me the ring."

I handed it his way. "Will you, Emma North, give me the immense honor of calling you my wife, of listening each night as you snore beside me, and of waking each morning as you come apart squeezing my cock in your perfect pussy?"

Scoffing, I shook my head. "Yes."

Standing, Rett placed the ring, sliding it down the fourth finger of my left hand before offering his palm, and adding, "And agree to submit to me whenever and wherever I say?"

Warmth intensified, creeping up my neck, undoubtedly filling my cheeks with pink.

"Emma."

Placing my hand in Rett's as the diamond sparkled in the lingering sunshine, I hopped off the window sill, my bare feet finding the floor. "I'm working on the second part."

A kiss came to my hair. "I know you are." Letting my hand drop, Rett stepped toward the door, the one to the hallway leading to the rest of the house, and turned back. "One day, Emma, if you want a giant wedding or one on top of a fucking volcano, it's yours. Today is about legality."

I turned toward the window, noticing the dimming light of dusk as the fountain's colors became more prominent. A smile came to my face as I turned back to my fiancé. It wasn't a term I could use for long. "Rett, I know it won't really be a ceremony, but could we say the vows or whatever the judge does in the courtyard? It doesn't have to be a sterile signing of papers, does it?"

His gaze went from me to the window and back. "I don't see why not."

Before he was gone, I remembered my earlier question. "Wait, why am I wanted for questioning if it isn't about you?"

"Can you trust me a little longer?" He paused. "No...can you trust me forever?"

*Forever.*

*Could I?*

I wanted to, more than anything else.

"I'm working on that too," I confessed, the memory of what Rett had said after he'd saved me from Kyle's men lingering in my thoughts. "Rett?"

His hand was on the doorknob, yet he craned his neck, bringing his sexy dark eyes my way. "What?"

"What about me? Will you ever trust me?"

His lips formed a straight line and he made a quick nod. "No one said marriage didn't have hurdles. I'm working on that, too."

My question scared me, but I had to ask it. "Tell me that I didn't ruin it...forever...when..."

"No, Emma. Nothing is ruined forever. We have our whole lives to work on all of this together." His forward motion stopped. "Oh, I almost forgot. Miss Guidry is bringing you a dress. You don't need to wear it, but she insisted that you deserved the option. She'll be up soon."

Running my fingers through my long hair, I knew that there was no way I'd be ready for my wedding in thirty minutes. I didn't care if it was only a judge; it was my wedding. "Rett, give me an hour."

He looked at his wrist and back. "Not a second more."

As the door closed, I realized his last proposal was what I needed, a reminder of what we've shared. Every night since the night I followed him to his room, we'd ended up in his bed. There have been other locations such as the back of the sofa, on the rug in front of his fireplace, and against the wall to name a few. It was as if that night opened a floodgate that neither one of us was ready to close.

Hurrying to the bathroom, I started the shower and

began opening drawers and pulling cosmetics and hair supplies to the counter. For only a second, I caught the blue eyes of the woman in the mirror. There was no confusion as to who she was, unlike the night Dr. Dustin had been with me.

I spoke to her. "We're getting married."

We both smiled as I stripped my casual gauze skirt down my legs and pulled my t-shirt over my head.

## EMMA

The knock came only minutes after I'd stepped out of the shower. My body was dry, but not my hair. I hesitated, wondering if it was Ian. There was no way it had been an hour. What if Rett had changed his mind on giving me more time?

With a large towel wrapped around me, I went to the door and opened it a crack.

Miss Guidry's smile was infectious. "Oh, Miss Emma. This is the answer to prayers."

In her hand and draped over her other hand was a long bag, containing what I assumed was the dress Rett had mentioned. While I couldn't see it, I had the feeling it was a real wedding dress. I opened the door wider, "Please come in."

She stepped in slowly, her eyes darting in all directions.

"Are you all right?" I asked.

Miss Guidry nodded fast as her hazel eyes glazed over. "I haven't... you know this was Miss Marilyn's suite. It holds so many memories." She took a deep breath and turned toward me. "I'm sorry, Miss Emma. The voices are loud."

Gently, I laid my hand over her arm. "May I look at the dress?"

The change of subject worked. Miss Guidry's smile was back as she hurried toward the bed and laid out the bag. "Now, I know you must think I'm a loony old woman..." She spoke as she unzipped the long bag. "You see, there's no greater honor than having your daughter wear your wedding dress."

Crossing my arms over my breasts as my hair dripped down my back, I bounced on my toes, waiting to see what she was unveiling. It was like an unexpected holiday surprise.

"Your momma never married, but planning a wedding was another of her dreams."

"That makes me sad," I confessed.

"No, don't be sad. That's not what today is about. You see, Miss Marilyn never had a daughter and well..." Miss Guidry turned and looked at me. "...she would be right honored if you'd consider wearing her dress."

*Rett's mother's dress?*

I fought an onslaught of emotions as I asked, "Do you think it will fit?"

Miss Guidry left the bag and walked toward me. Her

hazel gaze scanned and calculated as she did one circle and then another. Her voice lowered to a whisper. "You are a bit more endowed, if you know what I mean, but I promised her we'd try. May we try?"

"May I see it?" As soon as I asked, I realized how ungrateful that may have sounded. "I want to try."

"We don't have a lot of time," she said. "Now you go dry your hair. It's beautiful down, but if you want to wear it up, Miss Marilyn's veil is attached to a crown." She lowered her tone back to a whisper. "They aren't real diamonds, but they're beautiful. The one on your finger, she cherished that ring."

"I thought Rett said it was his grandmother's."

"It was. His great-grandmother's." Miss Guidry's head shook. "She was a strong woman." Her eyes twinkled. "She *is* and it took her some time, but she approved of Miss Marilyn too. She woke me one night and made me go tell Miss Marilyn." Her smile returned. "That's why I didn't wait to tell you Miss Marilyn's thoughts."

I looked down at the ring, silently scolding myself for thoughts I'd had of looking at more modern settings. When I looked up, Miss Guidry had the bag completely unzipped. What I saw took my breath away. "Oh, it's so pretty." I stepped forward, peering down at the intricate pearls and beadwork upon the bodice.

"I believe the white has yellowed," she said disappointedly.

"No, it's perfect. I always imagined an ivory dress."

That was exactly what Miss Guidry needed to hear. The spring was back in her step as she shooed me toward the bathroom. After my hair was dry and the towel was replaced with the white robe, I turned as Miss Guidry knocked on the doorframe and peeked in. "I used to help Miss Marilyn with her hair."

"Would you like to come in?"

As she entered, I took a seat on the stool near the makeup table and turned toward the mirror. For a few moments, she stood quietly running a brush through the length of my hair as I applied a primer and soft powder foundation. Each swipe was slow as she held handfuls of hair over her palm.

"Her hair was dark like Mr. Ramses," Miss Guidry said as her gaze met mine in the mirror. "Yours is more like your momma's." She seemed to struggle for a moment, finding the words. "I should apologize. Miss Marilyn was upset with me."

"She was? Why?"

"When you asked if she liked your momma, she wanted you to know, she didn't *dislike* her. It was that Miss Marilyn had her position to maintain, like you will. Some of what Mr. Ramses does, like his daddy before him did, isn't fit for mixed company. However, the Ramseses and Boudreaux have always been accepted. And with that acceptance comes responsibility and choices."

I watched Miss Guidry as she brushed my hair to

silky smooth ringlets wrapping around her wrinkled hands.

She continued to speak, "Well, I promised her that I'd explain what I meant." Our eyes again met in the mirror. "Miss Marilyn didn't really know your momma, and for that she wants you and her to know that she's sorry."

Swallowing the emotion the sound of her voice invoked, I began to focus on my eye makeup. Layer by layer, I added eye shadow, eyeliner, and mascara. I'd made an effort to appear date-worthy for Rett's and my dinners, but our wedding seemed the occasion for a little more dramatic style. It was as I was staining my lips that Miss Guidry took a step back.

"Miss Marilyn is right; you are the spitting image of your momma. Lordy, Jezebel in Marilyn Ramses's wedding gown."

I spun around. "If you don't think I should wear it—"

"Oh no," she interrupted. "I think you are just what the spirits have been waiting for. You're going to do so many things, Miss Emma, things your momma has planned. Mr. Ramses, he's smitten. I've never seen him like this and it's no wonder. No man can resist what you have."

"What do I have?"

She crouched down near my feet, her hands on my knees. "Honey, you have the power of a siren, the beauty of an angel, and fate has landed you in a place where you can do what couldn't be done before." Her tone grew more determined as her cadence slowed. "It shows in your eyes. You promise me that you'll use what fate is handing you? The spirits of all the families are watching and counting on you. Your momma's plans aren't done. The time is right. Miss Marilyn knows you will protect her son."

With each of her phrases, the determination in her voice, a weight fell a little harder on my shoulders. "I don't know what any of that means."

Miss Guidry stood and turned back to my hair. Her tone was completely different, back to carefree. "If you have some combs and hairpins, we'll have you ready to take your crown."

"What did you mean?" I asked as I pulled the implements she'd requested from one of the drawers.

"Your hair will look beautiful with the veil."

I watched Miss Guidry, wondering if she knew what she'd just said about me protecting Rett. He was the one who promised his protection. As she worked, I mulled over everything she'd said. As I did, I had a similar sensation of the one I'd had entering Rett's suite, of being a small piece of a bigger plan. The way his suite and the furniture within dwarfed me, I was tiny, a doll in a big house, waiting as someone moved me from room to room.

"What do you think?" she asked.

I wasn't sure how much time had passed or where

my thoughts had gone, but when I turned, my hair was piled upon my head in a loose bun, and long spiral curls hung down over my ears and shoulders. I lifted my fingers to her creation. "You did a wonderful job."

"Two more things," she said, hurrying from the bathroom. When she returned, the crown in her hand sparkled and a long train of organza followed. Reaching into the pocket of her apron, she laid on the counter the earrings Ian had brought to me a month ago. "These were Mr. Ramses's grandmother's. Something old. The dress is borrowed." She tipped the crown showing a small row of sapphires. "And something blue."

"The earrings are heirlooms?" I asked, shocked that I'd never realized they had sentimental value above their worth.

"Yes." She laid the crown on the dressing table as I secured the earrings.

"Do you think we should try the dress before the veil?" It was then I remembered Rett's time limit. An hour, not a minute more. "Miss Guidry, how much time do we have?"

"Mr. Knolls isn't here yet, so we're still good."

Together we stepped into the bedroom. The dress was beautiful, magnificent, stunning—every adjective I could use to describe it. I let out a sigh. "I don't know how to put it on."

She reached for my hand. "Now, with what you have" —she nodded toward my breasts— "and the sheer back, I don't think you'll be able to wear a bra. If we'd had more time, we could have gotten you something..."

My painted lips pursed. "Rett said I could have a real wedding one day. This one is just for legal purposes. Maybe it's silly for me to get all dressed up. I should save Mrs. Ramses's dress for later."

"You only have one wedding, Emma. Mr. Ramses can give you another ceremony, but this is the day you are to be wed. Shouldn't it feel special?"

I nodded as my smile returned. "All right. Let's do this."

Miss Guidry removed the dress from the cardboard form and arranged it on the rug. As I began to remove the robe, I had a sudden bout of bashfulness at my nakedness beneath. Rett had kept his word that panties were nowhere to be found. Warmth crept up my neck to my cheeks. Miss Guidry must have seen.

"Miss Emma, I've been dressing Ramses women for longer than you've been alive. Never you mind, we'll do this quick," she said with a wink.

Dropping the robe to the floor, I stepped into the circle. Miss Guidry lifted the bodice as I placed my arms into the sleeves. Sheer material accented with lace and pearls created cap sleeves. Together we tugged and pulled. The pearl-beaded bodice with the scooped neckline fit snuggly, but it did fit. Slowly Miss Guidry completed a long line of hooks and eyes followed by pearl buttons going down my back. The full tulle skirt with the lace overlay was fit for a princess and complete with a short train.

I stood in front of the long mirror in the closet, again questioning the woman in the mirror.

Miss Guidry's hand came to my lower back. "Mr. Ramses is a lucky man."

There was something about a wedding—even one hastily put together in an hour—that made me emotional. The reflection grew blurry as I smiled. "I think I might be lucky too."

We both startled at the knock on the outer door.

Miss Guidry handed me a lace handkerchief. "Now, you don't want to mess your makeup." She grinned. "I promise to do enough crying for all of us. Let me tell Ian that we're almost ready." She grinned. "You still don't have the crown and veil."

I wasn't sure how I'd forgotten that.

"I'll go to the dressing table."

Before I did, I surveyed the shoes on my rack and selected the nude heels I'd worn the first night Rett and I dined in the courtyard. Back at the dressing table, I slipped on the shoes. In the mirror I saw something amiss in Miss Guidry's expression. I spun toward her. "Is there a problem?"

"No, no. Just the spirits." She situated the crown on my head and secured the veil with the combs. As we both looked in the reflection, she hugged my shoulders. "You really are an answer to prayer, Miss Emma. I know you will do great things."

I laid my hand over one of hers. "Thank you for making this special, and please tell Miss Marilyn that I promise to do my best as Rett's wife."

Miss Guidry stepped around and offered me her hand. With a squeeze, she said, "She trusts you. Now, let's go."

# EMMA

*J*an was waiting at the door to my suite. "Miss North."

"Not for long," I replied with an anxious smile.

He lifted his arm. "If you don't mind me saying so, miss, you look beautiful."

"Thank you, Ian."

"May I escort you?"

I hesitated at the threshold. "Aren't we forgetting the blindfold?"

"No, miss. Mr. Ramses said that since soon this will be your home, it's time you saw more."

A genuine smile spread across my face as I placed my hand in the crook of Ian's arm. Miss Guidry followed, appointing herself in charge of the trains. The one on the veil and the one on the dress came together beautifully. Together, the three of us walked down a long hallway. I had known from Rett's and my dinner outings that the journey from the new suite wasn't as complicated with as many turns as the journey from the third floor.

As we came to a stop at the top of the main staircase, I had the sensation I'd been here before. What I'd missed with my eyes covered was the majesty of the beauty before me. Down a dozen or more stairs was a landing, the place where the staircase changed direction. At that spot, the ceiling went up to the second story and in the far wall was a spectacular stained-glass window filled with reds and gold. I stood for a moment, taking in the Ramses family crest. It was the same as the courtyard, made out of intricate craftsmanship.

"It's beautiful," I whispered.

Ian smiled my direction. "Mr. Ramses will be pleased that you approve."

My heart raced as we began to descend the first half of the staircase. As if on cue, outside lights beyond the window illuminated, sending colorful projections through the air. Colors danced before our eyes and upon the plastered and paneled walls and onto the rug below, as if we were walking through a kaleidoscope.

Ian stepped deliberately, careful to avoid the wide skirt while helping me navigate the beautiful dark wood staircase. We came to a stop at the landing, turned toward the final staircase, and my breath caught at the sight of the man below.

An hour ago, Rett had said this was a simply a legality, basically the signing of a paper. And now, he was dressed in a formal tuxedo, standing at the bottom of the staircase with one hand behind his back, and his dark gaze only on me.

With each passing second, I sensed the way he scanned me, viewing the lovely dress Miss Guidry had provided—his mother's dress—while also seeing beneath it, to the me underneath. I could now do the same thing of him, strip away the custom-fitted tuxedo and picture every indentation and muscle, knowing the way they felt over me and against me, as well as the way each one strained when he found his own pleasure.

I basked in Rett's change of apparel and appearance, from his gelled, combed-back and wavy dark mane and freshly shaved cheeks, all the way to his shiny Italian loafers. In between, the black tuxedo accentuated his toned torso and wide shoulders. With a white shirt, his white bow tie was undoubtedly meant to match my dress.

The beauty of the home around me and the grandeur of the foyer, tall front doors with leaded glass, the wooden arched entrances to other rooms, and the ornate large crystal light fixture all disappeared as I focused only on Rett.

Once Ian and I reached the bottom of the stairs, Rett smiled as he bowed our direction. Bringing his hidden hand forward, my fiancé presented me with a small bouquet of white gardenias, their stems secured with a light blue cloth. It took me a moment to realize the cloth was the blindfold from our first dinner. I lifted the bouquet to my nose, inhaling their intoxicating aroma that blended with my perfume and Rett's cologne.

I looked up at the man who had provided me with the real wedding he'd said wasn't necessary. "Thank you."

As Rett extended his arm, I moved the bouquet to my left hand and placed my right on his lower arm. Lowering his volume, Rett spoke as he led me down a hallway beside the stairs and away from the front of the house. "You are stunning. One day, I'll give you the ceremony you deserve."

Two members of Rett's staff opened the solid double doors leading to the courtyard. As it had been the first night we'd dined, the trees glistened with small twinkling lights, soft music filled the air, and the fountain's illumination reflected off the pebblestone paths, filling the space with colors.

I turned to Rett. "I don't need another ceremony. This is amazing."

My response was genuine. What had been created in a short time was so much more than I imagined an hour earlier...ever.

Rett lifted my hand from his arm and kissed my knuckles before placing it back in the crook of his elbow. When his dark eyes met mine and his lips curled into a smile, I believed the fairy tale. It was the one that little girls tell themselves only to grow up and discover they were only stories. Except at this second, it wasn't fiction. It was real. I saw the promise of forever reflecting in his brown orbs. The agreement we'd made had developed into more than a deal with a man who claimed he was the devil. It surpassed his facade. I wasn't marrying the devil but the man I'd come to know Everett Ramses to be.

While Rett was the man who brought me into a world I didn't know existed, he was also the one who saved me when I faltered and the one who understood my needs. That wasn't only sexual; it was emotional and mental. Rett knew what I needed to once again feel safe and to restore my belief in all he'd promised to provide. The Rett I'd come to know made me smile at the sound of his deep voice and brought me pleasure that was beyond anything I'd ever imagined. He also accepted my imperfections while pushing me to try new things and extolling my strengths when I did.

Following the pathway around the greenery, the fountain came into view. Standing before it was an older gentleman, tall, much like Rett, with thinning white hair and a lean stature. As Rett and I came to a stop before him, I had no misgivings about what we were about to do.

"Emma," Rett said, "this is the honorable Judge McBride of the New Orleans parish. While I'd originally asked him here to simply witness the two of us sign the marriage certificate, he's agreed to provide us with more of a ceremony."

"Thank you," I said to the older gentleman.

"It's my pleasure." Small lines formed around his eyes as his warm smile grew. "Your future husband can be quite persuasive."

Grinning, I looked up at Rett and back to Judge McBride. "I have to agree."

"Before we start," the judge said, "I feel that I have to ask a few questions."

There was no reason for his prelude to make me nervous, yet it did.

"Go ahead," Rett said, giving his approval.

"While I've known Mr. Ramses for most of his life," the judge began, "you, Emma are new to New Orleans. I feel the need to ask if you have any misgivings or reasons for not wanting this legal union to proceed."

Tears teetered on my lids as I looked around at the sparkling lights and down at my hand on Rett's arm. Shaking my head, I met the judge's stare and replied, "None at all, Judge McBride. I couldn't be happier to marry Rett...Everett Ramses."

The judge lifted a small card. "I see here on your ID..."

My eyes opened wider. I hadn't laid eyes on my ID since the night at the restaurant when I showed it to a waiter to get a Hurricane.

"...that your name is Emma Leigh O'Brien. How would you like me to address you during the ceremony?"

The last month ran through my thoughts, a highlight reel on fast forward. Everyone in Rett's employ addressed me as Miss North or Miss Emma. I hadn't used the name O'Brien since I checked into the Drury Plaza. "Just Emma would be fine."

Judge McBride nodded. "And Mr. Ramses?"

"Everett."

"Lastly, do we have our witnesses?"

"Ian Knolls," Rett said as Ian stepped forward. "And...?" Rett looked at me.

Releasing Rett's arm, I turned to find the one person I would want to be my witness. Her head was down and she had a handkerchief dabbing her eyes. "Miss Guidry?"

Immediately, her face snapped upward, and her hazel eyes settled on me. "Oh, Miss Emma, it would be an honor."

Moving the bouquet to my other hand, I reached back. When Miss Guidry reached me, she squeezed my hand. "The spirits are pleased."

"I do believe we're ready to begin," Judge McBride said. "And I've been told that as soon as we complete this ceremony, the marriage certificate is waiting in Mr. Ramses's front office." He looked from Ian to Rett, to me, and lastly to Miss Guidry. "I will need all four of your signatures. And then" —his focus was on me and Rett— "you two will legally be husband and wife."

Smiling at one another, Rett and I nodded and turned back to Judge McBride.

"Now, Emma, please hand Ruth your flowers so you and Mr. Ramses can hold hands."

*Ruth?*

I'd asked Miss Guidry to be my witness without knowing her first name.

Once I'd done as the judge asked, Rett and I turned toward one another, brought our hands together, and Judge McBride began. This was obviously not the judge's first ceremony as he spoke for a few minutes about marriage. While Rett's proposal hadn't extolled his undying love, Judge McBride talked about that and more as the key elements of marriage.

The first component he mentioned was love.

I had to wonder if Rett had given him parameters to meet or if Rett too was surprised to hear what the judge had to say. Judge McBride said that love wasn't something that needed to be searched for—it was. It wasn't brought to life nor could it die. Love lingered, waiting for its opportunities. It could surprise even its staunchest critics, as the seeds of everyday commitment took root and grew. It didn't travel a fast track or even a slow one. Love could come out of nowhere like a freight train bursting from the darkness or it could appear over time, such as the brightening of the morning sky as the sun burns away the fog.

The second piece to marriage was patience.

My painted lip disappeared beneath my teeth and

warmth filled my cheeks as I coyly peered up at Rett, wondering if he was thinking about some of the same things crossing my mind.

"Patience," the judge said, "is the ability to endure difficult circumstances in the face of disappointment and the tolerance of provocation and the ability to respond with kindness."

"To be *nice*," I whispered.

Rett squeezed my hand.

The final subject he mentioned was trust.

I couldn't help but replay the conversation from earlier in my head. Rett had asked me to trust him, not only today or regarding this marriage, but forever. It had been as I'd answered that I realized I wanted the same from him. I'd made a mistake, but I'd done as he'd said and learned from it. As we stood together, my hope was that we'd spend the rest of forever doing as we'd both said—trying.

"Do you have vows you'd like to say to one another?" Judge McBride asked.

I blinked my eyes as the wedding dress suddenly felt too tight. It was that sensation of being asked to do a speech in front of the classroom when none had been prepared.

"We didn't discuss it," Rett answered. He gently squeezed my fingers as his gaze met mine. "But I'd like to give it a try."

"Like your proposal?" I asked with a smirk.

"A little less personal." He winked. "Emma, it is an

honor to have you as my wife. I believe it's fair to say that I won't be the easiest of husbands. I've been told I lack some of the virtues that have been mentioned tonight, and yet fate had a plan. Thank you for promising to see where fate leads us and for making me the luckiest man, tonight and forever."

*Forever.*

I looked to the judge and back to Rett. "I guess it's my turn." I inhaled as the bodice pulled tight. "You, Everett Ramses, came into my life like a hurricane, which I suppose is appropriate for New Orleans. I think we've also learned that I won't always be the easiest of wives, but as long as we *both* promise to keep trying, to never give up on one another or ourselves, I believe we can fulfill fate's plan. I am willing to spend my forever trying as long as you're by my side."

His forehead came to mine as his deep whisper ricocheted through me. "I will never leave your side, nor you mine."

"Do we have rings?" the judge asked.

"I don't." It was the first time I'd thought about a ring for Rett.

"I do," my fiancé said, pulling something from his pocket. "May I have your left hand?"

I lifted my hand as he gently held my fingers and removed the large diamond he'd placed earlier in the day. "I'm good at a lot of things, Emma, but this isn't one of them." He changed out the solitaire diamond for a diamond-studded platinum band. And then he placed the single diamond ring over the band. "When I was a boy, my mother tried her best to instill some understanding into a determined young man. She'd bore me with stories. Now, I realize how valuable those stories were." He looked over at Miss Guidry. "Maybe she knows she succeeded." His gaze came back to me. "One story my mother would tell was about these rings. She would say that anyone can propose; it's a simple question. However, the act of marriage was never simple. It required commitment. That is why the band is worn beneath the engagement ring, closer to your heart as a reminder to the wearer that working for something you value is worth the effort." His sheepish smile made my insides twist. "I want you, Emma. I hope you decide every day that I'm worth the effort."

The judge hadn't given us the go-ahead, but that didn't stop us. Nodding, I lifted my arms around Rett's neck as he leaned forward and our lips met. We'd shared more passionate kisses, but at the moment, I didn't think we'd shared a more meaningful one.

"And there we have it," Judge McBride said. "By the power invested in me by the state of Louisiana and the parish of New Orleans, I pronounce you husband and wife, Mr. and Mrs. Everett Ramses."

Rett's gaze glistened.

"Emma Ramses," I whispered.

"Praise be," Miss Guidry said. "The spirits are dancing."

"Will you stay for dinner?" Rett asked Judge McBride after he shook his hand.

"Another time. As you know, this invitation came on my schedule rather unexpectedly. Let's go sign the certificate and the two of you can enjoy your first meal as husband and wife."

# EMMA

*A*s the solid doors to the house opened and we all progressed toward Rett's front office, the soft music and Miss Guidry's excitement mixed with loud voices coming from down the hall. Rett's and Ian's posture changed, our steps staggered, and Miss Guidry reached for my hand.

"Oh no," she said, "Mrs. Ramses, come with me."

Judge McBride seemed confused.

"You too, Judge McBride," Miss Guidry said, trying to lead us back to from where we'd come.

I tried to make sense of what could be happening as the mixture of concern and anger radiated from my husband's being.

The voices were close, near the grand staircase in the foyer.

It didn't make any sense.

*Who would be in Rett's home—our home?*

Henri, one of Rett's men, came around the stairs. "Mr. Ramses, I'm sorry. They demanded to wait for you. They have been checked and are free of weapons."

*They?*

*Weapons?*

"Ramses." The loud call came from beyond our view.

Rett turned to me. "Emma, go with Miss Guidry. She'll take you upstairs another way." He looked at Judge McBride. "This won't take long."

I reached for Rett's arm. "Will you be safe?"

"Yes, and so will you. Go."

Miss Guidry seized my hand and tugged me back toward the courtyard. Before we could get another step, the loud voice called again.

"Ramses. Where is she? Your man is telling the truth, we're not armed. Come meet me like a man."

My fingers flew to my lips as I pulled away from Miss Guidry. I knew that voice. I'd grown up with that voice. For eighteen years we'd lived under the same roof until he left for college.

"He's really alive."

"Emma, go," Rett commanded.

"No. Kyle said he isn't armed. You won't let him hurt me." I didn't even consider he was now going by a different name or what his men had done. He was my brother, Kyle O'Brien.

Rett seized my arm. "Not like this, Emma. Go."

I pulled my arm away. "I may be your wife, but I can make my own decision."

We both pivoted near the end of the staircase. In the large foyer staring back at us were two men. No introduction was necessary for either. One was the man I'd thought was my brother. The other was the brother of the man in the picture Rett showed me when I first arrived. While his brother Greyson had died, by the evidence before us, Liam Ingalls was very much alive.

I sucked in my breath as my eyes opened wide.

"Fuck, Emma," Kyle said, "tell me you didn't marry him."

My tongue faltered, forgetting how to speak as I stared at my brother. This was New Orleans; maybe he was a ghost or one of Miss Guidry's spirits. However, I knew he wasn't, and neither was the boy-turned-man beside him who'd taken my heart. Liam Ingalls had taken more than that. It was then I realized Rett had a pistol in his hand pointed at the two men.

With the large light shining down in the foyer, I scanned them both. With the same color hair and eyes as me, I again questioned if Kyle and I were biologically related. Liam was Kyle's polar opposite. Where Kyle was golden blond like me, Liam's hair was dark like Rett's. Kyle's eyes and mine were both blue. Liam's were a mesmerizing green. I'd seen those eyes in my dreams and nightmares. After my family's death, images of his eyes brought on tears with the memory of how Liam told me he was leaving and that there was no future for us.

"Emma, go the fuck upstairs," Rett growled as he lifted his pistol.

He wasn't the only one holding a gun. Ian and Henri both had barrels pointed at Kyle and Liam and in the distance, I heard others coming.

Kyle lifted his hands above his head. "I told your man I'm not armed, Ramses, and neither is Ingalls. There's no need to kill us like you did Greyson."

Rett took a step forward. "Unarmed, it will make it easier to kill you both."

"No." I had found my voice.

"Emma, upstairs."

"You married him?" Liam asked.

"Why are you here?" I asked as memories of my abduction came back. "Leave. Listen to Rett and get out."

Kyle spoke with his hands now on top of his head. "Em, I came to tell you what's happening and to free you from...him."

*Free.*

"I'm not captive, Kyle. I live here." The lies I'd lived with for too long gave me strength. "Furthermore, why would I go with you? I'm Rett's wife. You lied to me. God, Kyle, you're alive. You let me think...let me mourn...."

The male image of me took a step closer, but stilled his steps as all the guns lifted, still pointed his direction.

Kyle shook his head. "I'm sorry I couldn't tell you before now. I didn't mean to hurt you, Em. I meant to include you. That's why I hired Underwood to watch you and get you here to New Orleans."

My gaze went to Rett and back to Kyle. "You hired Ross?" I lifted my hands to the side of my head. "I can't believe you, Kyle." I looked to Rett and shook my head. "I'll ask Ross."

"Sis, he's dead," Kyle said. "Your husband had Underwood killed. Ramses not only had him killed, he had Underwood's death ruled a suicide."

"What?"

"He's lying, Emma," Rett replied. The volume of his voice rose. "Now get the fuck out of this house."

"Are you going to slaughter me in front of my sister?"

"You know she isn't your sister."

"Is it true?" I asked Rett in disbelief. "Is Ross dead?"

More men had gathered, coming from where I wasn't certain. In a mere matter of minutes, they outnumbered Kyle and Liam by at least eight to two and also eight firearms to none.

"Get them out of here," Rett ordered.

As a large man I didn't know gathered Kyle's arms behind his back and my brother struggled, he said, "Em, you look just like her and so do I. There's so much you need to know. Ramses is a liar and a murderer. Come with us."

There were too many things going through my head. "Where have you been for four years?"

"It's a long story."

I took a step toward him. "You talk about Rett, what about you and your men? Did you know what your men did to me?" Tears infiltrated my words. "You let them hurt me. Get out of this house and out of New Orleans."

"Get him out," Rett yelled.

Kyle's head shook back and forth as he was dragged toward the door. "I don't know what you're talking about. I've been trying to find you. It was the court filing this afternoon for the marriage license that tipped us off."

"Your men," I said, explaining, "the ones who took me."

"No, Em." Kyle's expression was puzzled. "My men would never touch you. I wouldn't allow it." His blue eyes went to Rett and back to me. "Listen to me, don't stay here. Come with us and learn the truth."

As I tried to grasp what Kyle was saying, Rett's men surrounded him and Liam, pushing them through the double front doors out into the yard and driveway. As the volume rose, the air filled with Rett's orders.

*If Kyle's men didn't take me, who did those men work for?*

My stomach lurched at the only other possibility—one I couldn't bear to entertain.

Rett stood in the doorway. Turning, he looked back my direction. "Emma, remember what you said."

My expression must have asked for clarification.

His dark stare bore down on me. "You said you'd trust me."

There was too much.

I needed clarification.

I hurried past Rett and yelled to the outside for Kyle. "Who is *us*? Who should I listen to, you and Liam?"

Kyle turned my way.

"You've both lied to me."

Kyle's voice came over the dull roar of the commotion. "Em, I'm sorry. I'll tell you the truth. Us doesn't mean Liam. You should listen to our mother."

"She died," I reminded him.

He fought as he was being pushed into the back seat of an SUV.

"Kyle," I called one last time.

"Jezebel, Em. She's alive and I swear, she can explain."

As Kyle disappeared into the SUV, I stepped back and back, into the foyer. My heart beat in overtime against my breastbone as the bodice of the dress grew tighter. Breathing became difficult as too many thoughts clouded my mind and I sank to the stairs, sitting on the bottom step. Beyond the double doors, Rett's men disappeared, taking away my brother and my first love.

When Rett stepped back inside, he closed the double doors. With a deep breath, he ran his hand over his hair, pushing it back from where it had become disheveled. I looked up, wondering who was telling me the truth.

Rett offered me his hand. "Come, we need to sign the marriage certificate."

I didn't budge. "Jezebel is alive?"

He nodded. "I never said otherwise."

I shot to my feet. "So you lied by omission?"

"Miss Guidry told you. She speaks of Jezebel in the present tense." He reached for my hand.

I pulled it away. "She speaks of your mother in present tense too."

Rett continued to offer his hand.

Refusing to reach for it, I held the banister and stared back up to his gaze. "Tell me who took me."

"I have their names if you want to see them. Their identities are irrelevant, Emma. I won't allow them or anyone else to harm you. They're dead."

*Just like Greyson and now Ross.*

The finality of his statement cooled my skin. "Who hired them?"

"Emma." Rett took another step closer, his presence dwarfing me as his timbre slowed. "Come with me, now."

Applying pressure to my teeth, I stared at the man before me.

*Had Rett told me the truth?*

*Was he truly the devil?*

The earlier noise from all the commotion was gone;

a new blistering silence rang in its place as Rett's nearly black eyes narrowed. "Now, Emma. You agreed to this deal with me."

I had, and yet as my grip tightened on the top of the banister, I was unable to move forward.

The doorway to the room right off the foyer caught my attention. The tall doors were opened. The room within glowed with golden light from a large chandelier above. The furnishings were like something out of a museum or a palace. Standing guard were more of Rett's men. Ian was within, speaking with Judge McBride. Miss Guidry was also there, her head shaking as she added to their conversation.

As my presence lingered, it was as if I were one of her ghosts, present, but unable to affect the world around me.

Rett's voice lowered, piercing the fog of illusion. "Emma."

My chin snapped toward him, yet my lips didn't move.

His earlier emotion was gone. In its place was Rett's usual demeanor, one of superiority and power. It was as if the world was once again in his control. For a moment that dominance had been in jeopardy but no longer. His firm lips curled in victory as his arm wrapped around my waist and tugged me toward the room with the others.

With Rett's warm breath near my ear, to others his attention might have appeared gentlemanly. However, as goose bumps coated my skin, I heard what others couldn't: the underlying growl and warning.

"Remember my rule."

My feet began to move in unison as we neared the room.

"You promised, angel. Judge McBride is waiting with our marriage certificate, and you will sign."

You have reached the end of DEVIL'S DEAL.

Don't miss the dramatic finale of Rett and Emma's story in ANGEL'S PROMISE.
Purchaset your copy after June 29, 2021.
You won't want to miss a second of the Devil series.

If you haven't read Rett and Emma's meeting, download the entirety of "Fate's Demand" now for free on all electronic platforms.

## WHAT TO DO NOW

LEND IT: Did you enjoy DEVIL'S DEAL? Do you have a friend who'd enjoy DEVIL'S DEAL? DEVIL'S DEAL may be lent one time. Sharing is caring!

RECOMMEND IT: Do you have multiple friends who'd enjoy my dark romance with twists and turns and an all new sexy and infuriating anti-hero? Tell them about it! Call, text, post, tweet...your recommendation is the nicest gift you can give to an author!

REVIEW IT: Tell the world. Please go to the retailer where you purchased this book, as well as Goodreads, and write a review. Please share your thoughts about DEVIL'S DEAL on:

    *Amazon, DEVIL'S DEAL Customer Reviews

    *Barnes & Noble, DEVIL'S DEAL, Customer Reviews

    *iBooks, DEVIL'S DEAL Customer Reviews

* BookBub, DEVIL'S DEAL Customer Reviews
*Goodreads.com/Aleatha Romig

# BOOKS BY NEW YORK TIMES BESTSELLING AUTHOR
# ALEATHA ROMIG

## DEVIL'S SERIES:

### FATES DEMAND

March 18

### DEVIL'S DEAL

May 2021

### ANGEL'S PROMISE

June 2021

## THE SPARROW WEBS:

## DANGEROUS WEB:

### DUSK

Releasing Nov, 2020

### DARK

Releasing 2021

### DAWN

Releasing 2021

## WEB OF DESIRE:

### SPARK

Released Jan. 14, 2020

### FLAME

Released February 25, 2020

### ASHES

Released April 7, 2020

## TANGLED WEB:

### TWISTED

Released May, 2019

### OBSESSED

Released July, 2019

### BOUND

Released August, 2019

## WEB OF SIN:

### SECRETS

Released October, 2018

### LIES

Released December, 2018

## PROMISES

Released January, 2019

# THE INFIDELITY SERIES:

## BETRAYAL

Book #1

Released October 2015

## CUNNING

Book #2

Released January 2016

## DECEPTION

Book #3

Released May 2016

## ENTRAPMENT

Book #4

Released September 2016

## FIDELITY

Book #5

Released January 2017

## THE CONSEQUENCES SERIES:

### CONSEQUENCES

(Book #1)

Released August 2011

### TRUTH

(Book #2)

Released October 2012

### CONVICTED

(Book #3)

Released October 2013

### REVEALED

(Book #4)

Previously titled: Behind His Eyes Convicted: The Missing Years

Re-released June 2014

### BEYOND THE CONSEQUENCES

(Book #5)

Released January 2015

### RIPPLES

Released October 2017

## CONSEQUENCES COMPANION READS:

## BEHIND HIS EYES-CONSEQUENCES

Released January 2014

## BEHIND HIS EYES-TRUTH

Released March 2014

## STAND ALONE MAFIA THRILLER:

## PRICE OF HONOR

Available Now

## THE LIGHT DUET:

Published through Thomas and Mercer Amazon exclusive

## INTO THE LIGHT

Released June, 2016

## AWAY FROM THE DARK

Released October, 2016

## TALES FROM THE DARK SIDE SERIES:

### INSIDIOUS

(All books in this series are stand-alone erotic thrillers)

Released October 2014

## ALEATHA'S LIGHTER ONES:

### PLUS ONE

Stand-alone fun, sexy romance

May 2017

### ANOTHER ONE

Stand-alone fun, sexy romance

May 2018

### ONE NIGHT

Stand-alone, sexy contemporary romance

September 2017

### A SECRET ONE

April 2018

## INDULGENCE SERIES:

### UNEXPECTED

Released August, 2018

### UNCONVENTIONAL

Released January, 2018

### UNFORGETTABLE

Released October, 2019

### UNDENIABLE

Released August, 2020

# ABOUT THE AUTHOR

Aleatha Romig is a New York Times, Wall Street Journal, and USA Today bestselling author who lives in Indiana, USA. She has raised three children with her high school sweetheart and husband of over thirty years. Before she became a full-time author, she worked days as a dental hygienist and spent her nights writing. Now, when she's not imagining mind-blowing twists and turns, she likes to spend her time with her family and friends. Her other pastimes include reading and creating heroes/anti-heroes who haunt your dreams!

Aleatha impresses with her versatility in writing. She released her first novel, CONSEQUENCES, in August of 2011. CONSEQUENCES, a dark romance, became a bestselling series with five novels and two companions released from 2011 through 2015. The compelling and epic story of Anthony and Claire Rawlings has graced more than half a million e-readers. Her first stand-alone smart, sexy thriller INSIDIOUS was next. Then Aleatha released the five-novel INFIDELITY series, a romantic suspense saga, that took the reading world by storm, the final book landing on three of the top bestseller lists. She ventured into traditional publishing with Thomas and Mercer. Her books INTO THE LIGHT and AWAY FROM THE DARK were published through this mystery/thriller publisher in 2016. In the spring of 2017, Aleatha again ventured into a different genre with her first fun and sexy stand-alone romantic comedy with the USA Today bestseller PLUS ONE. She continued with ONE NIGHT and ANOTHER ONE. If you like fun, sexy, novellas that make your heart pound, try her UNCONVENTIONAL and UNEXPECTED. In 2018 Aleatha returned to her dark romance roots with SPARROW WEBS.

Aleatha is a "Published Author's Network" member of the Romance Writers of America and PEN America. She is represented by Kevan Lyon of Marsal Lyon Literary Agency and Dani Sanchez with Wildfire Marketing.

facebook.com/aleatharomig
twitter.com/aleatharomig
instagram.com/aleatharomig

Made in the USA
Columbia, SC
31 October 2021

48051491R00178